Some
Maintenance
Required

Some Maintenance Required

Marie-Renée Lavoie

Translated by Arielle Aaronson

ARACHNIDE

Titre original: *Les chars meurent aussi* par Marie-Renée Lavoie
Copyright © 2018, Les Éditions XYZ inc.
English translation copyright © 2022 Arielle Aaronson

First published as *Les chars meurent aussi* in 2018 by Les Éditions XYZ
First published in English in 2022 by House of Anansi Press Inc.
www.houseofanansi.com

House of Anansi Press is committed to protecting our natural environment. This book is
made of material from well-managed FSC®-certified forests, recycled materials, and other
controlled sources.

House of Anansi Press is a Global Certified Accessible™ (GCA by Benetech) publisher. The
ebook version of this book meets stringent accessibility standards and is available to students
and readers with print disabilities.

26 25 24 23 22   1 2 3 4 5

Library and Archives Canada Cataloguing in Publication

Title: Some maintenance required / Marie-Renée Lavoie; translated by Arielle Aaronson.
Other titles: Chars meurent aussi. English
Names: Lavoie, Marie-Renée, 1974- author. | Aaronson, Arielle, translator.
Description: Translation of: Les chars meurent aussi.
Identifiers: Canadiana (print) 2022016102X | Canadiana (ebook) 20220161038 |
ISBN 9781487007737 (softcover) | ISBN 9781487007744 (EPUB)
Classification: LCC PS8623.A8518 C5213 2022 | DDC C843/.6—dc23

Cover image: Katy Lemay / Trevillion Images
Text design and typesetting: Marijke Friesen

*House of Anansi Press respectfully acknowledges that the land on which we operate is the Traditional
Territory of many Nations, including the Anishinabeg, the Wendat, and the Haudenosaunee. It is also
the Treaty Lands of the Mississaugas of the Credit.*

**Canada Council
for the Arts**   **Conseil des Arts
du Canada**   ONTARIO ARTS COUNCIL
CONSEIL DES ARTS DE L'ONTARIO
an Ontario government agency
un organisme du gouvernement de l'Ontario

With the participation of the Government of Canada
Avec la participation du gouvernement du Canada

*We acknowledge the financial support of the Government of Canada through the National
Translation Program for Book Publishing, an initiative of the* Action Plan for Official
Languages—2018–2023: Investing in Our Future, *for our translation activities.*

Printed and bound in Canada

MIX
Paper from
responsible sources
FSC
www.fsc.org   **FSC® C103567**

Some
Maintenance
Required

1

"My dad died."

It wasn't possible. I'd seen him just two days earlier. Surely a death this sudden had to come in the form of crumpled metal, an explosion of runaway tumours, or a stray bullet. It had to be some long, complicated story, not a few hushed words spoken through a doorway one beautiful summer morning.

"I don't understand..."

"Heart attack. He was out on a boat."

Tickers often stop without warning, so I guess it was possible after all. Just like in books, death in real life can strike lightning-quick and tidy.

The authorities had already repatriated Sonia's dad's remains, stuffed like a sausage into a body bag before he even got a taste of the legendary wild beauty of Anticosti Island. Ten years of scrimping to save up for the fishing trip of a lifetime had come to an abrupt end in the oblong hull of a rowboat. No one ever warns you about the dangers of an overdose of beauty.

"Sonia's staying home today!" barked an aunt who had rushed over to manage the crisis. My friend was yanked back inside, and the door slammed on my eager-ness to know more. Only a puff of cigarette smoke slipped outside, like a toxic ellipsis hanging in the air.

I wound my way through the back alleys that led to the hospital parking lot, where I knew my mother would still be at work inside her little shoebox. As I walked towards her, the notion of such an unexpected, merciless death expanded in my mind, like those tiny grow-in-water foam dinosaurs. I sped up to keep the idea from swallowing me whole.

Suzanne smiled at me from across the lot as if we hadn't seen each other in weeks, though we'd eaten breakfast together two hours earlier. From the moment I was born, I've been a source of perpetual wonder to my mother. If I so much as breathe, she'll start gush-ing over my amazing talent for living. A casual smile can smooth anything over and cheer her up for hours. From the beginning, she forgave me for everything I was not and would never be; in the distorting mirror of her heart, I'd mastered whatever I tried before I'd made so much as an attempt.

In the seventeen square feet where she'd spent her days for almost as many years, a ray of sunlight shone through the small round window my father had cut into the southeast wall of her parking booth, a porthole overlooking a sea of cars whose shimmer was lost in all the grime.

"You got here just in time, sweetheart. I really need to pee!"

"Okay, you can go now."

"Why the long face, kiddo?"

"Go pee first."

"What happened?"

"Mom, just go to the bathroom."

Whoosh! She slid the main window of the booth closed, cutting us off from everything—cars, her need to pee, my urge to beat back the tragedy. That was the magic of her booth: when the window was closed, it was a fully soundproof wooden cube that existed beyond the laws of time and the outside world.

"Out with it!"

"It's Sonia..."

"What's wrong with Sonia?"

"Her dad died."

There was a momentary pause as she opened her eyes wide.

"He didn't! He *didn't*! I don't believe it... Wasn't he going out fishing?"

"He had a heart attack."

"Dear Lord!"

"On the boat."

"Goodness! Who told you?"

"Sonia."

Her arms sagged like deflated balloons. Big, hot tears slid down my cheeks, joined paths under my chin, and splattered the tip of my shoe. She held me close to shoulder some of my pain.

I wasn't mourning Sonia's dad, of course. I'd only known him as the tip of the head that stuck up past the armchair in the living room. I was crying for my now half-orphaned friend. And because it dawned on me that my father was old, too, and that his heart could give out at any moment. Death has a way of making us selfish.

Outside, cars forced to wait in a single-file line by the barrier blocking the exit had begun a chorus of honking. People don't like hospitals and hate parking lots; they utterly despise hospital parking lots.

"Go pee, Mom."

"Okay. Go ahead and collect from this bunch, they're getting antsy. I'll be quick."

I was just a little girl the first time I took over the booth. There was no one to guard the lot in my mother's absence, so she became a prisoner of the four walls.

It never bothered her that much; she kept a chamber pot under the counter for emergencies. But as soon as I was old enough to make the trip from our apartment on my own, her working conditions vastly improved: she let me hold down the fort while she ran in to use the hospital bathrooms. I'd developed a habit of coming by whenever I could, more than once a day if possible, to chase away the image of my mother squatting over a porcelain vase inside her wooden box at the parking lot entrance.

As a girl, I'd had to lean halfway out through the window to grab the parking vouchers and cash and to give change. Now, I was big enough to sit on the padded barstool and stick my grownup arm out to collect from customers. It was more of a stretch than an effort. But my mother was shorter, and reaching out for each transaction strained her back.

From the outside, no one could have guessed the tiny refuge sitting in a field of cracked concrete was the paradise my mother had made of it. The booth no longer looked anything like the handful of boards the hospital had originally thrown together. It had been well insulated, thanks to my father's handiwork, and two space heaters maintained a pleasant temperature in winter (as long as the door wasn't opened too often). The walls were covered in pictures of exotic landscapes torn from Club Med magazines, and she'd brought in spider plants and African violets to brighten up the place and purify the air and the view. My mother especially loved the violets; she said the word *African* gave them a tropical feel. A fold-up seat taken from the Montreal metro — long story — had been screwed into the wall opposite the window, allowing for visitors. Well, a visitor. And a big glass jar full of the stuff of children's dreams sat next to the register, ready to offer bursts of delight in the form of chewy caramels.

The hospital administration hadn't balked at her price tag once they'd realized that the other employees' issues seemed to resolve themselves whenever my mother was at her post. The one time she thought she'd lost a ticket, it was found a few days later in an abandoned car that had to be towed. After that, they'd created a permanent position for her.

It would be a mistake to think that, just because she was shut up year-round in her snug little nest, my mother never went anywhere. She read novels, heaps of novels. So many novels that the moment she opened one she could gauge with surgical precision how long it would take her to finish. "This one's forty pages an hour, so it'll take me . . . eight hours and forty-five minutes. I'll be done by tomorrow afternoon if you want it." She read enough novels to unabashedly discuss travel with anyone, convinced that her literary experiences could measure up to those of actual globetrotters. After all, her voyages came coupled with a profound knowledge of the joys and sorrows each place held. She may not have seen Notre Dame Cathedral in Paris with her own eyes, but she was no stranger to the secret passions it hatched and the sad souls that lurked in its shadows. Everyone knew Italy was the cradle of the Renaissance, but not everyone could fall in love at the mere sound of a shoe hitting the wet Venetian stones after the rain.

Five minutes later I'd cleared the line and rewarded myself with a piece of black licorice. I was eyeing my mother's most recent library loans when she came running back.

"Okay, now, spill! What a crazy story — I still can't get over it. How could he just up and kick the bucket like that?"

"I dunno, that's all she said."

"No details?"

"No, there were people over. She couldn't leave."

"Poor kid. It's tough, losing your dad at eighteen."

"Yeah. He was pretty old though."

"Couldn't have been that old."

"Sonia's brother is twenty-five."

"He was probably in his fifties, like me."

"Older than that."

"Doubt it."

My mother's notion of one's fifties was quite elastic, spilling generously over into the next decade. It was like she was trying to make up for the forty-three years she'd spent waiting for me.

"Weren't you supposed to work at the bakery today?"

"No, I switched shifts with Isabelle. Sonia and I were gonna hang out at the Old Port."

"You could go without her?"

"Meh."

"With a book to take your mind off things."

"I don't feel like it."

"I understand. But take this one anyway, I just finished. It takes place in Santa Barbara. Can't go wrong with California. Six and a half hours."

I might have taken it if the cover hadn't been so hideous. The hazy outline of a girl reaching for some sort of glittering stream was set against a psychedelic backdrop in a failed attempt at magical undertones. Far too new-agey for my taste. A small line of cars had formed behind the gate in the few seconds we'd been talking.

"I'm gonna head out, Mom. You're busy, it's the lunch rush."

"That's some news! I still can't get over it."

"Want me to bring you something to eat?"

"Thanks, doll, but I made a sandwich. Until I see her next, give my condolences to Sonia. I'll check the newspaper for the viewing and the funeral."

As she spoke, she took tickets, punched them, calculated the amount owed, communicated this to the driver by a show of fingers — one, two, three, four, five dollars — and put away both the ticket and the money. Someone had been smart enough to adapt the parking fare to the number of fingers on the human hand.

"Viewing of what?"

"The body."

"Why?"

"So people can see it."

"Yuck! Why would they want to do that?"

"The family needs to see the body. Helps with the grieving process."

"But that's gross. He's dead!"

"The morticians will do him up nicely. He won't even look dead."

"How'll they do that?"

"By pumping out all the blood, I think. Maybe the guts, too."

"Ugh, that's so gross..."

"They fill the veins with something else, so you can't tell. The casket stays closed if the body's too banged up. But he had a heart attack so he should be okay, unless he was out there a while before they found him. Sometimes, when you're exposed to the elements like that..."

"He was in a boat."

"Yeah, but the birds could've gotten to him. They like pecking at the eyes..."

"MOM!"

"Sorry. It was in a movie I saw."

"Okay, I'm leaving."

"See you later. Oh, hang on! Tell your dad about Sonia. I think he'd just found a car, actually."

"For Sonia?"

"No, for her dad."

"What do you mean?"

"I dunno, he wanted a car. But tell your dad so he doesn't hold on to it. Here one day, gone the next. I just can't believe it..."

I knew I'd find my dad at home, since he always came back for a quick nap on his lunch break. Before dozing off, Serge would shovel down a few pieces of "toast" smeared with butter and mustard (he never actually bothered with the toaster, but I guess calling them slices of bread sounded less like a meal). Since my mother often remarked that this was more of a quick fix than a lunch, he'd come to believe it and told anyone who'd listen that he owed his health to a preventive approach to nutrition.

I rounded the bend in the alley and spotted Cindy, the ragtag little girl who'd recently moved into the neighbourhood. She was perched on an outlandish pair of high heels that must have belonged to her mother. With her hair in tangles and a filthy dress falling off her shoulders, she was sticking one grubby hand into a bag of ketchup-flavoured chips and furrowing the dirt behind her like a miserable little tractor, sending up clouds of dust. Before dipping her hand back into the bag, she made sure to wipe both sides of it on her dress, cleaning it up for the next round of chips.

The first time my mom brought Cindy home it was to give her socks. She'd been walking around, sockless, in the middle of winter, and the powdery snow that had fallen overnight slipped silently into her unlaced sneakers. She couldn't have weighed more than a sack of onions. My mother lured her in with some red licorice, and she scarcely hesitated. It was that easy. She tried to get Cindy to talk as she slipped on socks, a scarf, mittens, and a toque, but the feral child dodged her questions with grunts, as if the words scratched her throat on their way up. Cindy just stood there, transfixed by the bowl of fruit sitting on the counter, until my mother handed her an apple. Then she ran off with her spoils, feet dragging in the snow.

Over the next few days, Cindy came back and stuck her dirty little nose right up against the kitchen window. We'd let her in to peruse the selection of fruit, and she'd choose the one she wanted. After a few weeks, she even managed to sit down to eat it. Convincing her to wash her hands took a lot longer. I had a hard time checking the dark thoughts I harboured for her parents.

"Our hands are tied, sweetheart. You want to call the DYP, but what would that do? They're up to their eyeballs in worse cases, lemme tell you. She'd get carted around from foster family to foster family, and for what? We've both seen her dad. Not a bad guy, just not the sharpest tool in the shed…"

Her father pumped gas at the Sunoco down the block. Any attempts by the chain to impose a well-groomed aesthetic by way of a uniform were utterly thwarted by the man's ungainly proportions. His bowling pin–shaped body defied all standards of beauty and all styles of dress; summer or winter, no outfit could ever quite cover the bulge of his woolly abdomen and the milky white of his lower back. He was so doughy it was tough to pick out his shoulders in the mountain of flesh that served as a torso. And you could easily get lost in the fathomless void of his haunted gaze. In my dad's words, a case of wet spark plugs. I'd only ever gotten an *okay by me* when I went to their apartment to see if Cindy could come over.

Her mother? She was like a wild animal holed up in her den. A complete mystery to us. Our best guess was that she just didn't know where the door was.

"They don't take care of her, but at least they don't beat her. And if we call the cops, they'll just move. People like them are shifty, they avoid neighbours like the plague. Nah, it wouldn't help a thing. I hate to say it, but the kid's gotta save herself. She trusts us, and that's not a bad start. I mean, she isn't coming here for the fruit..."

I made a slow approach, one day at a time. Whenever Cindy was around, I would develop a sudden craving for fruit. I treated her like a house of cards, resisting the urge to touch her, to ask the slew of questions that was eating me up inside. Instead, I watched and waited until she was ready. The nervous tics that wracked her body calmed as her grimy fingernails tore through peels to release the fruit's sweetness. I laid down paper towels to contain the carnage. It was through a drizzle of blood orange that she announced she wanted to go to "Messico."

"Mexico?"

"Yeah."

"Why?"

"It's hot there."

"You've been?"

"Nope."

"Who told you about Mexico?"

"Nobody."

"Okay."

"So, can I?"

"Uh...no, it doesn't work like that."

"Why not? I wanna go!"

"Plane tickets are expensive, and it's really far."

"Fuck you!"

The little hand she'd so calmly placed on the table only moments before swept away everything in its path. She narrowed her eyes at me and ran out to the stairs in a fit of disappointment. I was overwhelmed by her faith in us; she'd come to believe that if she so much as asked, she would receive.

It took three days of sulking before we saw her wild mane of hair at the window again. I waited until she was inside before saying, in the most neutral, least didactic voice possible, "Cindy, we don't say 'Fuck you.'" I waited for her to spit in my face and throw herself back down the stairs, but she just stood there, glued to the linoleum, staring at the basket of fruit. I wasn't going to push it by asking for an apology. Not this time. We might get there one day.

"You can have whatever you want."

"This one."

"Say please."

"Peease."

"Take it."

"What is it?"

"A kiwi."

"S'ugly."

"But it's good. And you can't always find them at the grocery store. Hang on, I'll cut off the skin for you."

"It's got fuzz onnit."

"You don't eat the fuzz."

She didn't look up at me once the entire time I spent torturing the poor kiwi. The notion that she had to make amends for something kept her quiet. My mom had been right: Cindy would end up saving herself. She'd managed to intuit a line, albeit a blurred one, between right and wrong. It was a start.

"We can pretend to go to Mexico."

"Nope. I don't wanna."

"Eat your kiwi, then come to my room."

On the floor, in a patch of sunlight streaming through the window, I'd laid out two bath towels and some cushions for our heads. My clock radio was playing mood music. I'd dug up some sunglasses, two cans of ginger ale with bendable straws, and a fan to simulate the ocean breeze. I'd even brought in the fake plant from the living room to act as a makeshift palm tree. If we rolled up our sleeves and pant legs, we could almost imagine we were in bathing suits. I was the first to lie down.

"That's not Messican music."

"It might come on later."

"I don't buhleev you."

"Sit down, the sun's blazing hot."

"This isn't Messico."

"Okay, well, you're missing out."

I'd been baking in the sun for two minutes when I felt her lie down next to me. She put on the sunglasses, took

a sip of ginger ale, and pouted for another five minutes
before falling asleep. It took a moment for her waiflike
frame to settle. First the nervous spasms subsided, then
her filthy little fingers with their chipped and bitten nails
relaxed, and finally her mouth went slack, which trans-
formed her body into an echo chamber that amplified
the sound of her breathing in long, regular waves. We'd
made it to the sea. At the end of the day, as I would
soon discover, Cindy was just a normal little girl left to
her own devices. When her body couldn't take it any
longer, she succumbed to sleep. The big purplish rings
that stretched from her eyes to the top of her cheekbones spoke volumes.

After a successful maiden voyage, we often returned
to Mexico. From there we'd hop down to the Galapagos
Islands to see the giant tortoises. We visited the
Caribbean, Spain, and the pristine whiteness of the
Greek islands, followed by lots of hot and exotic places
we'd probably only ever see in our heads. With a few
pretty sentences, we'd sail through the most dizzying
time zones. Our destinations matched the Club Med
ads my mother had given us for inspiration. And since
Cindy almost always fell asleep, the real adventure lay
in the preparations. My mother helped set the stage,
describing in great detail how it felt to lie on a deserted
beach somewhere in Fiji — the place where all the secre-
taries from her Harlequin novels who were "beautiful

on the inside" ended up. I would fine-tune the rest once we were lying down.

"Look at the ocean. There's nothing but water, as far as the eye can see. No mountains, no houses, no streets, no cars, nothing. Just emptiness for miles. If your eyes are real good, you can even see the Earth curve way out in the distance..."

"Pff! Thassa lie."

"Just calm down, relax, and let go. There's nothing bothering you. Everything's good. It feels good, too, like in the winter when your hands are freezing and you run them under warm water..."

Cindy rushed over when she saw me coming back from the booth that day, dragging her feet so she wouldn't lose her shoes.

"Those are way too big for you. You're gonna break your neck."

"No way, they fit perfect."

"Your mom won't like it if you take her shoes."

"They're mine!"

"They're yours?"

"They used 'ta been hers, but now they're mine."

"You have chip crumbs all over your face."

She swiped at her face with the frayed hem of her dress, revealing a faded pair of underwear, a translucent belly streaked with blue veins, and dark nipples that would one day become breasts, if all went well.

"Don't lift up your dress like that! I can see everything."

"Hey! Quit yelling or I'm gonna leave."

"Okay, bye. I'm going to . . . Africa."

"NOOO! I wanna come!"

"Come on, then. I'll carry you upstairs, otherwise you'll hurt yourself."

"What's Affica?"

"*Africa.*"

"What is it?"

"It's a continent."

"Pff . . ."

"Know what a giraffe is?"

"Yup."

"A lion?"

"Yeah."

"Africa is where giraffes and lions live."

"Is it hot there?"

"Really hot! You'll see."

My dad was polishing off his second butter-mustard slice when we walked into the kitchen. I didn't bother making a big speech to explain Sonia's dad's sudden death. "Heart attack" was enough to get the point across.

"He was pretty young to die."

"Whatsa hardattack?"

"It's something old people get."

"Who found him in the rowboat?" My dad wanted to know. "A park ranger or another fisherman?"

"No idea. We didn't have time to talk."

"Bet it wasn't pretty..."

"Whatsa rowboat?"

"A small boat."

"Strange though, boating's not hard on the heart..."

"I wanna go inna boat!"

"But Cindy, we're going to Africa."

"I'll bet he worked like a dog just to haul it into the water. And then the minute he put his feet up and cracked open a cold one..."

It was tragic but also strangely beautiful to picture the red explosion of his heart painting a fresco against the dappled shades of green and brown.

"Just found him the deal of the century, too. A real clean Hyundai Pony for three fifty. Not a ton of horse-power, but perfect for the city."

"That's so cheap!"

"In great shape, too. Lady-driven."

"What about me?"

"What about you?"

"I could buy it."

"Me, too! Me, too!" Cindy was practically hopping.

"What for?"

"For anything! Driving to work, going out, shopping..."

"Taking me to Messico!"

"The bus stop is two blocks away. And I give you rides half the time."

"Yeah, and this would give you a break."

"Owning a car's a real headache. The three hundred bucks isn't the problem. It's all the gas, the repairs..."

"You can help me with those."

"Licence and registration, insurance..."

"I'm a girl, it'll be cheap."

"Ima girl, too, Laurie!"

"It all adds up."

"When did you get your first car, Dad?"

"That was different."

"Why?"

"Yeah, why issit?"

"That Pony's not right for a girl. It doesn't even have power steering."

"I don't care about that. Plus, I'll be going off to university soon."

It was a low blow, but I couldn't help it — I knew the single, noble word had the power to rekindle my parents' hopes and dreams. Whenever we talked, my mom pronounced it with reverence, savoured it, rolled it around in her mouth as she pictured the wonders it embodied, packed with American clichés: majestic stone buildings, cathedral libraries lined floor-to-ceiling with books, classrooms overflowing with Einsteins, and a shower of mortarboards flung about by graduates with bright futures ahead of them. She never dared open the science books I brought home from college, just placed a solemn palm on their covers as if they were sacred texts to be handled with care. Her passion almost scared me. My dad heaved a long sigh, defeated before he'd even begun to fight.

"You havin' a hardattack, too, mister?"

"Don't be silly."

"I dunno, you're old."

"Me? Old? I'm a spring chicken!"

"Your hands an' face are all wrinkly."

2

Behind the microphone, the priest rolled his *Rs* around hollow platitudes whose soporific echoes washed over the crowd gathered in the church's sombre hall. His puffy pink hands made slow, delicate circles in the air, rising and falling along with his voice. Pricking his sausage fingers with an X-ACTO knife might have deflated them and freed the bloated digits from further paralysis.

"Réjean would have been delighted to see us gathered here today... in the house of the Lord, our God... our guide... as we send him off to his final resting place... Réjean had a zest for life and was surrounded by the love he so cherished... Réjean, who loved the outdoors, has now left this world behind for a better one, in the company of our Lord...doing what he loved most in life...in perfect harmony with nature, may he rest in peace..."

It seemed to me that Réjean had died at the exact moment he wanted to live. I bet he would have traded one of the best days of his life—his wedding, the births of his children, the night the Canadiens won the Stanley Cup—for a chance to spend just one full day on the island of his dreams. I didn't see much to celebrate in such an ill-timed tragedy; his trip had been cut short before he'd even had time to hunt or catch a single fish. With eyes closed and hands clasped, the devout were busy imploring the almighty guy up above to save them from such an ending; everyone else was making a mental note to go get a damn electrocardiogram. I decided that if working in mysterious ways meant blocking arteries at the worst possible time, this Lord must be a petty and cruel god.

"Réjean, our brother...who sacrificed all his life for his loved ones..."

This was the same Réjean who never let Sonia's mom get a job. Who had been too brainwashed with the ecclesiastical hogwash of a bygone era to risk sparing her from domestic servitude. I mean, who knows? She might have earned a living, become independent, found her own way to happiness. And he had always refused to pay for Sonia's jazz ballet classes, claiming they were a "damn waste of time." Réjean—I hadn't even known his name until the funeral—had sacrificed, yes, but only within limits he had carefully set himself. Regardless, the priest immortalized his soul with his broad brush, laying on the virtues so thick it painted over even the most troublesome cracks.

"...today, the Lord has welcomed home a loving husband and caring father...surrounded by the tender embrace of friends and family, in life as in death..."

"Where are you going?"

"Outside. I'll just be a minute, Mom. I need some air."

"*Now?*"

"I can't breathe."

"Your father must be out there."

"...let us grant him the honour, dear brothers and sisters of God's great church...to depart in peace, as he would have wanted..."

It was more fun to do the Stations of the Cross backwards, with Jesus regaining strength the closer you got to the door. I dipped my fingers in the font to cool off my neck.

On the concrete walkway that led to the front courtyard, I found my father smoking quietly, one hand in his pocket, feet shoulder-width apart for more stability, standing among the guys from the garage where he worked. Most of the guys who had shown up for the funeral preferred to wait outside, claiming they were allergic to incense or host dust. The starched collars of their too-clean clothes made their necks itch.

"Well, looky who's here! S'over already?"

"No, just the sermon."

"Christ . . . I can't take it."

"Me, neither."

"Too much sittin' there, listenin' to a guy in a nightgown who gets off on Jesus . . ."

No one was offended by the blasphemy; Bob had gone to a parochial school, the term itself charged with a darkness we avoided stirring up at all costs. He'd never told us his story, but we could fill in the blanks from the unbridled hate that, over time, had taken root in his imaginary theatre as a carnival where saints and consorts played the clowns. The only one he spared was Mary Magdalene, because he had too much respect for whores. I watched as flasks of cheap gin traded hands discreetly. It was as good a way as any to receive communion.

"So, how's the body look?"

"I didn't go up. It grosses me out."

"I heard his face's yellow, all jaundiced-like."

"Who told you that?"

"Piston's wife."

"She saw him?"

"Came in earlier to decorate the altar. Smelled to high hell when they opened the caskets' what I heard."

"Bodies always smell to high hell."

Ron handed me his flask, and I took it. The fiery swig licked at my insides, loosening me up straight away. I thumped my chest to balance the pain on the inside and the outside.

"Better?"

"A little."

"So, big girl, how're ya likin' the Pony?"

"It's awesome."

The guys at the garage poked fun at the model name, which didn't exactly evoke power the way other car names did. I didn't see the problem: a pony is a horse. A small one. True, the car's pedigree wasn't all that impressive; any less horsepower and it could have doubled as a horse-drawn carriage. But blinded by love for my Pony, I could overlook anything—even its vague and unsettling colour, best described as "rust." It had a metal frame, four tires, a steering wheel, and it could drive on the highway. It suited me perfectly. And at no extra fee, my Pony protected me from the rain, played music, and even kept me warm in winter. It was more than enough.

An ambulance with its lights off was parked a few feet away. Clearly its services weren't needed at the moment.

"You're late to the game, boys. He's already dead!"

The guys thought they were hilarious. Ron started coughing like a tuberculosis patient. With his pale-blue eyes, he looked every bit the tragic hero out of a romance novel, knocking on death's door.

"We came for the sandwiches."

"Same 'ere."

"It's an open mass, right?" The paramedics didn't want to take any chances; they were close enough to death as it was.

"Seems it."

"We'll stick around, it could come in handy..."

With one arm dangling over the door, the paramedic looked at me and raised an eyebrow slit with a scar. A classic Don Juan move, used all too often by the men in my mother's books. I wasn't impressed.

"You guys gonna roll the coffin to the cemetery on a stretcher?"

"Sure, if they need a hand."

Someone rushed out of the church.

"Get in here! They're doing communion!"

We were rebels, sure, but only up to a point. If we ended up going to hell, it couldn't be through just any door. That minuscule slice of blessed bread would give the guys the strength to reject the rest of the Church. Sermons went in one ear and out the other, carefully sidestepping the canal's spiral staircase, but the molecules of the communion wafer became embedded into their flesh, instantly forgiving certain sins via divine osmosis. No bolder than the others, I followed them in. Mostly I wanted Sonia to think I'd stayed to the end. Right before the massive door closed behind me, I took one last look at the paramedic: he flashed me a magazine smile. Okay, fine, he was almost cute.

While everyone waited their turn in line to shuffle forward, the guys gave a brief refresher to Pichette, who hadn't set foot in a church since Grade two. He hadn't even been confirmed. His state of disgrace, coupled with the merciless teasing, had him almost worried. He'd come to church to eat tea sandwiches and wound up with an anvil on his conscience.

"Put your right hand underneath, you're gonna use it to receive the host."

"But that one's dirtier, I can't get the grease off."

"The priest'll say something, I forget what..."

"'The body of Christ.'"

"Ah, right. Then you say 'Amen.' All's there is to it."

"What's 'Amen' mean?"

"Who cares?"

"It means 'okay.'"

"Naw, it means 'thanks.'"

"Thanks for what?"

"For giving you the goddamn host."

"What if I take it with my left?"

"Then it's straight to hell, pal."

Everyone was in their Sunday best, going out of their way to present a dignified face for the funeral.

The women were sucked in, made up, teetering on four-inch heels; the men and children had washed their hair, or slicked it back. Sitting over to the left, one of Sonia's aunts on her mother's side was sporting a *yé-yé* star getup, with her lavender velvet pantsuit and matching hat jammed over her jet-black hair. The honourable citizens behind her couldn't see a thing, other than the priest's bratwurst hands whenever he held his arms wide. The grieving faces in the pews on the right, where Sonia's father's family sat, loudly disapproved. Nasty comments, whispered on all sides, ricocheted off the kneelers and pinged through the background noise. The priest drawled on in his booming monotone. *Goddamn sack of trash . . . Stick up your ass! . . . Gussied up like a whore . . . Constipated old fart!* Open war broke out at the funeral, Sonia would later tell me, when her mother and her grandmother began to fight over who was grieving the most.

"Losing a child's worse'n losing a husband."

"Easy to say when you still have a husband."

"I gave that child life."

"The man shared my bed for twenty-six years."

"You'll find someone else to share it, you never did have trouble in that department."

"You bitch! Some things never change!"

Sonia was wedged all the way at the end of the bench, her eyes puffy, her cheekbones swollen, her face ravaged. She couldn't care less about where she fit into the hierarchy of mourners — she wasn't ready to share her father with the dandelions. I tilted my head forty-five degrees and put my hands together, trying to give her a morale boost, knowing all I could do was mouth a heartfelt "I *love* the leather skirt!" From far away, it looked real.

I turned around and found myself inches from the priest, who was busy placing a thin slice of God into my father's knotted hand just steps from the casket. Inside it, a dead man was sleeping — a yellow man with red-currant lips lying in an armful of fake, garishly coloured flowers. A man with no hands. They had been covered by a shroud that attracted more attention than it diverted. Had they rotted? Had his body jettisoned them like autumn leaves once it realized the pump could no longer deliver the blood? Had they been cut off to make room for the embalming tubes?

"Miss? Are you okay?"

"Laurie? Laurie!"

Everything went hazy and I let myself fall, the need to lie down suddenly irrepressible. Muffled voices cut holes through my semi-consciousness. I could feel myself being lifted.

"Get outta the way!"

"They're parked out front! Hurry! Go get 'em!"

"I thought he looked a lil' creepy, too…"

"Maybe she forgot to eat, she's pretty skinny."

"They're all anorexics at that age."

When my vision cleared, the paramedic with the scar was smiling down at me, as if we were two lovers in a movie shot from above. It was the first time I'd seen grey-green eyes; they reminded me of worn-out car-battery terminals, or the roof of the Château Frontenac. *Beyond phenotypic limits*, my biology teacher would have said. I could see my mom behind Don Juan, her face a worried crescent moon. The image of Réjean's body suddenly rushed back to me, and I jumped.

"Whoa there! Relax!"

"Where's Sonia's dad?"

"Not here. We're by the entrance."

"Shit . . ."

"Don't move, I'm taking your blood pressure."

"I'm fine."

"I need numbers for the report, sweetheart."

"Okay."

"What's your name?"

"Laurie."

"I'm Fred."

"I want to get up now."

"Just give me two minutes."

He played with his little rubber bulb while I focused on the line of dust that ran all the way down my black pants. Church floors require maintenance, too.

"I think you should go home anyway. Are these your parents?"

It was hard to deny. Just behind him, close enough for him to feel their breath on his neck, my mother was folded into my father's arms, apoplectic with worry.

"Yes."

"Did you drive here?"

"Yeah. Even though we live three blocks away."

"Okay, Laurie, let's get you up. Hang on tight."

"You sure she doesn't need to go to the hospital?" My mother's eyes searched his.

"Don't worry, ma'am, there's nothing wrong with this woman."

Woman, not girl. He'd completed my resuscitation with princely tact. I decided his eyes were castle green, in the end.

"Lean on me, and don't let go until I say so. We'll walk together for a bit."

"Okay."

"One, two, three . . ."

That day, I walked out of church on the arm of a handsome stranger who only had eyes for me. It would never happen again, but it didn't matter. Perfect moments don't need to be recreated.

We traded the burial and tea sandwiches for the comfort of our front stoop. A warm, fragrant autumn breeze blew through the maze of bustling alleys. My mother insisted on staying "dressed" as long as her hair was already "done up"; a shampoo and set clashes with weekday clothes. One of the ladies in the neighbour-hood might give her a compliment. To increase the chances of being seen, she'd run a few perfectly unnec-essary errands. As for me, I made tracks for Hollywood with a Danielle Steel that nearly put me to sleep. After about a hundred pages, the holier-than-thou bombshell with a tea fixation started to get on my nerves. She could have easily snagged a glass of champagne if she'd only stuck out her hand. I went to grab something else, far from the pile of Steels.

Sonia dropped by to check on me as the sun was setting.

"Are you okay?"

"Yeah, I'm totally fine. I'm sorry."

"Come on, it wasn't your fault. But, uh…hello, paramedic!"

"Pff, he wasn't that hot."

"If I'd known, I'd have fainted, too."

"Way too old, though."

"Maybe we wouldn't be virgins anymore if we screwed guys like him instead of stupid idiots like Carignan."

We'd agreed that our wholly disappointing first times hadn't made a dent in our virginities. Since we hadn't enjoyed the experience, or even come close, it didn't count. The mechanical twitching of Kevin's pelvis against one of my body's most promising openings, if the literature was to be believed, simply didn't deserve such a grandiose name.

"What about you, how do you feel?"

"Meh."

"Your mom?"

"She and my stupid crazy aunts are still fighting like cats."

"The purple one's really something."

"You'll laugh, but she's the nicest. They're all stuck up on my dad's side."

"*Stick up your ass!*"

"You heard her say that?"

"Everyone heard her."

I'd missed a bunch of other gems, along with some lapel-grabbing over lunch that had almost degenerated into a fight: when the subject of money had come up, one of Sonia's uncles had called her cousin a *gold digger*—the ultimate insult. As with any good family, some members thought they were entitled to part of the life insurance for unpaid debts, services rendered, broken promises, and more. The usual pack of vultures descended.

"We're moving."

"What? Where?"

"Dunno yet."

"Why?"

"My mom wants a real house, with nobody on the sides and nobody up top. She's sick of living in a shithole."

"Your place isn't that bad."

"She wants a yard where she can sunbathe in peace."

"I hang towels over the balcony railings so no one can see me."

"I'm gonna need a car, too..."

And that was when Cindy decided to show up with her five-star pout. Her boat shoes were practically falling off her feet, and her grubby shorts and T-shirt matched the rest.

"Hey, little pickle!"

"Hey, big turd!"

She'd explained that it was a term of endearment. My mother had told me to cut her some slack.

"Whose shoes are those?"

"I'm hungry!"

"Go get a piece of fruit."

"I wanna samwich."

"You can't ask for stuff that way, Cindy, it's not polite."

"But I waaant one!"

"How do you ask?"

Then Sonia chimed in.

"I wouldn't say no to a sandwich..."

"You didn't eat after the service?"

"Just some macaroni salad. The sandwiches looked gross. They dyed the bread blue, my dad's favourite colour."

"Lau, I'm huuungry..."

"Go ask Suzanne and Serge if they want one, too."

"Can we get 'em from Pierrot's?"

Astride my Pony, with Cindy perched on her throne of phonebooks so she could "see up front," we picked up half a dozen extra-mayo egg-salad sandwiches and a few cans of spruce beer that we took out to the balcony of our apartment. The evening echoed with the sounds of clinking bottles and muffled voices spilling out from the jumble of not-houses. The neighbour's cat came to lick the lumpy sauce that dripped down Cindy's hands. Refracted through Sonia's earlier words, the apartment seemed to shrink around me, like something out of a Boris Vian novel. Her mother's new aspirations, bristling with a contempt not usually voiced, suddenly ate away at the spaces I'd always lived in but never truly seen.

3

On the scrap of newspaper the bakery manager was holding out to me, someone had made a big red circle around a job offer for an experienced waiter/waitress.

"It's not far, over on Boulevard Hamel. A five-minute drive."

"Me?"

"Of course, doll! Certainly not for me!"

"Why not?"

"I'm fifty-four, honey. There's not a restaurant in town that'd hire an old bag like me. I wouldn't last a day, anyway. Too exhausting."

"But I've never been a waitress before."

"You'll learn, like you did here."

"It's not the same."

"True, you'd make a helluva lot more. And you'll need it for school, your car, an apartment, all sorts of things."

"But it says 'experienced.'"

"Doesn't say what kind."

"Obviously it means waiting on people!"

"Unclear. Maybe life experience counts, who knows."

"It says to bring in a resumé today between one and three p.m."

"Uh-huh."

"I don't have a resumé."

"No big deal. You can give 'em the oral version today."

"But I don't have anything to put in a resumé!"

"Weren't you a counsellor for the day camp in the park last summer?"

"Yeah, but…"

"And didn't you work at a video store?"

"Yeah, for like two months. For an old pervert who paid me under the table."

"What about here?"

"Uh… we sell bread."

"Don't you have tons of qualities that'd make you a great waitress?"

"Pff…"

"You know you do. You're smart, you're a quick learner, you're organized, strong, nice, patient, brave, you're… hey now, we can't have any of that!"

A wave of pink washed over my face; I was touched. She squeezed my arm so I wouldn't melt on the spot.

"Don't cry or your eyes'll be all puffy."

"I get off here too late, anyway."

"Oh, just run over, we'll cover for you. No one'll know. Marie won't leave until you get back."

"You want me to go now?"

"Right now."

"Okay. But what if I don't get it?"

"Then at least you tried."

Ten minutes later, with sweaty hands gripping the life preserver of my steering wheel, I parked my econo-box in front of the empty restaurant. My legs were less enthusiastic about this opportunity to become a wait-ress, and it took a good ten minutes to get out of the car.

A woman with a tired smile greeted me kindly just as I was about to turn back. My heart was beating so loudly, I could scarcely hear the pan pipes playing softly over the speakers. I folded my arms over my chest so I wouldn't smudge the perfectly polished surface of the brass handrail.

"For one?"

"Uh...no. I'm here for the ad, the resumé."

"Ah. Give it to me, I'll take it to Carole. She's still here."

"I...uh...I don't actually have it."

"Oh? Not off to a good start, then."

"I know. Could I see the manager, anyway?"

"What for?"

"To tell her."

"Tell her what?"

"My resumé."

"You want to tell her your resumé?"

"I was at work when I saw the ad, and I don't keep a copy with me . . . it's at home, but I think I can . . ."

"Phew! You had me worried."

"Yeah, I definitely have one . . ."

"No, that outfit."

"Ah . . . it's the bakery uniform."

A mint green stunner trimmed with dusty-pink frills. The puffed sleeves added to its pontifical clownishness.

"Lord, it looks like it hasn't changed since the seventies!"

"Actually, this is the new one . . ."

"My God! Okay, come on. If you're not a good fit, she'll tell you herself."

On the way, we passed two servers finishing up their shifts. They both looked elegant in matching outfits: black pants, white shirt, black bow tie, black shoes; black apron tied at the waist, corkscrew hooked over change purse. Wow. Any humiliation I was about to suffer would be instantly vindicated if it led me to this classic image I yearned for myself.

"Carole? Sorry, it's just that I have a resumé here."

"You can give it to me."

"The girl wants to tell it to you, she doesn't have a paper copy."

"Oh! What time is it?"

"Ten to three."

"Okay, fine. Show her in. Thanks, Estelle."

I took a deep breath.

"Uh . . . hello. I don't have my resumé with me because I'm in the middle of a shift and . . ."

"What's your name?"

"Laurie."

"I'm Carole."

"Hello."

"You know your resumé by heart?"

"Yes and no . . . but I can basically tell you what's in it because I haven't had tons of jobs yet, even though I've always worked, ever since I was little. I shovelled snow for years, and then I did babysitting and stuff like that, a lot of times just to help out. I don't know why, but kids like me, maybe because I'm an only child, but that's a different story — although I bet it's good experience to work with kids, I'm really good at making them laugh. Speaking of that, I was a camp counsellor for a few summers at the local park. I've got a good imagination and tons of energy — my mom says I'm like the Energizer Bunny because I keep going and going. After that, I worked at a video store but my boss was, uh . . .

pretty demanding, and…anyway, I left pretty quick to go work at the bakery. One of my mom's friends recommended me, but I really proved myself. I'm a hard worker and I never complain, even when it's my turn to work the cash—you can't move a muscle the whole time because you're stuck in this little wooden cage they made just for working the register. I put the words on the cakes because they say I've got good handwriting, but I'm also strong enough to handle the baking sheets and big racks. They call me the great woman of the gospel, but I haven't read the Bible, so I don't really know who that is, but it doesn't matter. And I'm really patient, I'll do anything you ask, and I get along with everyone, and I'm really good with numbers. I take care of the register and sometimes I make the schedule and even do the sales reports, too. I have a real head for math, which comes in handy. I'm studying applied science at college and I don't know what I'll do with it, but I definitely won't end up working in a parking lot. Plus, I'm available nights and weekends…"

Carole raised a finger and opened her eyes wide. I was so nervous that I looked up at the ceiling, only to realize she was just asking to speak, like at school.

"Uh…yes?"

"You're really cute and you seem pretty sharp, sweetheart, but I already gave the job to Julie from the Red Lobster that just closed. I had about twenty-five people lined up earlier, and I didn't think anyone would come in at ten to three. So, the position is filled."

"Okay. Sorry, I didn't know."

"No, I'm sorry. I was in a hurry, and I didn't even have time to tell Estelle. I needed to get the new person trained as soon as possible, so I made a quick decision."

"Okay."

"Plus, you don't have any restaurant experience..."

"I know."

"Otherwise, I'd have put you on a waiting list in case anyone backs out. That's why I wanted to hear your resumé, anyway."

I ran away without a word, without a goodbye, my mortification magnified by the nonsense I'd spouted at lightning speed.

Safe in my rust-coloured Pony, I burst into tears. Puffy eyes be damned. Even better, I thought, since it might help ward off questions at the bakery. People would see that it hadn't gone well, and they'd leave me alone. It looked like I'd be stuck with the clown suit a little while longer.

I was just about to pull away when I saw Carole leave the restaurant and walk briskly towards me, waving.

"Wait!"

I scrambled to look busy as I shuffled through the pieces of paper lying on the passenger seat before I opened the door. The window had been jammed shut for some time.

"Look... you seem so earnest... I'm going to give you a chance. You've gotta start somewhere, eh?"

"Seriously?"

"But as a hostess. I can give you a few hours over the weekend. Not a ton, but things are always changing, hostesses never stay for long. You won't get tips like a waitress, but you might get your chance if a spot opens up. Hostesses often help out the servers, so it's a good opportunity to learn."

"For real?"

"What do you say?"

"Definitely! But are you sure?"

"I'm offering it to you... It's just a trial run, though. We'll see how you do, and we can decide later."

"Okay."

"Are you in a hurry?"

"Actually, yeah, I'm on the clock at the bakery and one of the girls is covering for me until I get back."

"No problem, go ahead. I was about to leave, myself. Come to my office on Saturday morning at ten. Go through the back door, the front will be locked. We'll do the paperwork before lunch and you'll shadow Estelle after that. Oh, and I'll need your social insurance number."

"Okay."

"Come in wearing straight-leg black pants, black

shoes, and a white shirt. I'll give you an apron and a bowtie. I've got everything in the back."

"It's the same uniform as the servers?"

"Yes, except for the colour of the apron."

"Wow!"

"Sound good? I'll see you at ten a.m. on Saturday?"

"Great!"

"What's your full name?"

"Laurie Gagnon."

"Okay. See you Saturday, Laurie."

"See you Saturday, Miss."

"Carole."

"Okay . . . Carole."

"Ah! Hang on, I almost forgot. How old are you?"

"Eighteen."

"Perfect."

She had spent the entire conversation crouched down to remain at my level, hands gripping my seat so she wouldn't lose her balance. To an outsider, it must have looked more like a marriage proposal than a job offer. I was even crying tears of joy.

When I walked into the bakery, the girls were pretending to be swamped with work so as not to pounce on me like they probably wanted to do. Lise was repositioning sandwich buns already perfectly stacked, Jacinthe was scrubbing the glass of the sparkling-clean display case for the eighth time that day, and Marie-Claude had momentarily left the register to help a customer choose a baguette that was perfectly baked — not too hard and not too soft, just perfect, fresh, there you go, miss, you won't be disappointed with this one.

"But the ones in the plastic bags are softer. They look much fresher."

"No, ma'am, those are the day-olds. The plastic makes 'em soft."

"Well, either way, I don't like hard baguettes that're all dried out. I like 'em fresh in the plastic better. And anyway, that's what plastic's for, to keep things fresh."

"The old fresh one it is!"

I stood in the middle of the room and smiled. Whatever was urgent stopped being so on the spot.

"Well? *Well?*"

"They'd already filled the position."

"What?!"

"Seriously?"

"But how? You got there before three."

"Don't worry, Laurie, honey, there'll be others."

"Restaurants are a dime a dozen."

"Not too disappointed, I hope?"

"Your eyes are all puffy. Were you crying?"

"It's nothing against you. If they filled the position, they filled the position..."

"True, it's all about the timing."

"Yeah, just bad timing..."

I raised my arms over my head in triumph.

"So I'm gonna be a hostess instead!"

"AHHH!"

"NO WAY!"

"ARE YOU SERIOUS?"

They jumped up and high-fived one another like they'd just won the lottery, the spontaneous burst of joy making them act like children. Seconds later, hands hastened to readjust hair, sleeves, belts. But as the jubilation left their bodies, it remained on their faces: they were really and truly happy for me. Theirs was a simple happiness, limited to the confines of a paycheque or the contours of a narrow reality, and they found it in them to wish this happiness on others. On me.

"You better come back and see us, duckie."

But they'd been through this before. Even as they said it, they knew I'd come by next week, and the one after, too, but soon my visits would taper off until they were just awkward. Later on, when our paths crossed by chance, effusive shows of affection would be reduced to a polite wave, hands lowering in tandem with eyes that wouldn't know where to look. The questions would move from the sphere of intimacy ("So, so, so, did you see Dave yesterday? What a cutie!") to the realm of census-taking ("Where do you live these

days? How many kids? How are your folks doing?").
After a time, with a deftness that would fool nobody,
we might even manage to cross paths without seeing
each other.

That day, I stopped by the hospital on my way home.
My mother wasn't at work, but her booth stood out
against the twilit sky. From a distance, only the parking
attendant's head was visible in the lighted window.
Not for the first time, the thought dawned on me that
I didn't want that life, didn't want to end up there.
That my mother's spectacular strategy for surviving
in her shoebox couldn't hide the fact that, when you
got down to it, her entire job consisted of monitor-
ing a barrier securing access to a parking lot. That
my idea of a real job had never squared with this
underpaid prison. That I had unwittingly established
a social hierarchy in which my mother occupied the
lowest rung. That I was frightened of this rung as if it
were a shameful disease. And that I was bewilderingly
ashamed of my fear.

. . .

A barefoot Cindy was waiting for me to see whether, as I often did, I'd brought home a handful of little Vachon snack cakes that had passed their best-before date. It hadn't even crossed my mind.

"That sucks, I really wanted one!"

"I know, kiddo, but you'll have to get used to it. I won't be working there much longer."

"Why not?"

"Because I'm going to have a new job."

"Why?

"Because."

"What're you gonna do?"

"I'll be a hostess at a restaurant."

"Pff…"

"Do you know what a hostess is?"

"Nope."

"It's the person who shows you where to sit."

She raised her chin and looked at me with big, wide eyes.

"That's stoopid!"

"No it's not, it's fun!"

"Pff…"

"What do you want to do when you're big?"

"What my dad does."

"Pump gas?"

"Nooo, *punt* gas."

"It's *pump*, with a *p*."

"Pff…"

"Stop huffing, you sound like an untied balloon. Come on, let's get a little treat at the corner store."

"A big treat!"

"Where are your shoes?"

"Summere."

4

"I never want to see you empty-handed! Pick up whatever you can — plates, utensils, napkins, trays, trash, ashtrays, you name it. Full hands in, full hands out, it has to become automatic. No empty hands."

Estelle ran the dining room as if she owned the place. A former waitress whom age had relegated to the role of head hostess, she knew that keeping her job depended on an excellent work ethic. As her body's machinery wore out, one part at a time, her movements lost their fluidity. Pain seeped in through every crack. She was an ageing woman in an enemy body. The artifice of her former beauty — her calculated slimness, freshly dyed hair, and neatly drawn lips — only accentuated the irreversible fact that her youth had slipped away from her.

I had to memorize the layout of the dining room, with its haphazard system of table numbers and sections. It was my job to greet the customers and show them to a table, evenly distributing the parties among the serv- ers' sections. But the tables near windows attracted as much as those near the bathrooms repelled, rendering the principle of fairness utterly futile. It was also my job to help serve and clear tables; seat and entertain chil- dren; wipe up the messes made by children and servers; run out to the neighbourhood shops to look for change; clean and restock the service stations, counters, and bar; dry the glasses and utensils; make / cancel / change reser- vations; and do a thousand other things that saved just about everyone's life. *Hostess* made it sound somehow glamorous; really, I was a jill of all trades responsible for solving everyone else's problems.

Carole almost never came into the dining room, much preferring the chaos of the kitchen. She firmly believed customers would rather be served a meal than three glasses of water and an empty apology from the manager. Surrounded by cooks and facing a bottleneck of orders, she would stand there frowning and ramping up the pace by clapping out a "Go! Go! Go!" She kept control over the kitchen with a no-nonsense attitude and barked out orders that were never challenged. Platters of lasagna, veal parmigiana, and pizza-caesar combos hurtled with stunning efficiency through the swinging doors until calm descended once again. Then she would wash her hands, crack a private little smile, and return to her sales figures, which she carefully manipulated until they reflected a profit.

A few months after I started, on a Thursday when I'd swapped sociology class for an extra lunchtime shift, Carole called me into her office and made three big announcements. She was pregnant. She would be taking a less strenuous administrative position at the chain's headquarters and would be replaced within the week by a specialist from Toronto tasked with maximizing productivity (despite her best efforts, the restaurant's performance remained disappointing). And she had recommended me highly for the position of dining room assistant manager.

"Me?"

"Yes, you."

"But..."

"You can make the schedules."

"I know, but..."

"I was told you thought the section divisions didn't make sense. You could make a few suggestions."

"Yeah, okay..."

"You're good with numbers. I've seen you do the girls' register."

"Only after I'm already punched out."

"I know, it's not a criticism. And Estelle likes you a lot."

"Well, yeah, what about Estelle?"

"I'd prefer it to be you, for now. But I haven't forgotten you want to be a waitress. Claude knows, too."

"Claude?"

"The big guns from Toronto."

"I don't know, I feel like . . . What about college? I'm in my last year . . ."

"We'll work it out so your hours don't change much. Claude will spend lots of time on the floor, it's part of his mission, so that'll give you more time in the office."

"The office?"

"You'll be an assistant manager, so you can use the office to do paperwork."

"Okay, but I'm happy just being called hostess. That's fine with me."

"No can do. If you don't have a title, the girls are going to walk all over you. When they find out you'll be making the schedules and assigning the sections, you're going to catch a lot of flak. You'll have to stand your ground. But Claude will have your back, don't you worry. He'll be the one to deal with the whiners and their little tantrums."

"I don't know . . ."

"And you'll need the title to get the raise."

"Raise?"

"Three bucks an hour."

"THREE BUCKS AN HOUR MORE?"

. . .

I didn't tell my parents the big news until the following morning because I didn't want to fire them up right before bed.

My father smiled and mumbled a string of *would ya look at thats*. Then he shook my hand and gave me a pat on the back before escaping to the garage. My mother put a hand over her mouth and began studying the patterns on the vinyl floor to regain composure. She started rattling off the problems such a sudden promotion could generate as a way of grounding herself — and me — in reality.

"You won't quit school, will you, love?"

"No, Mom. I'll still work nights and weekends, same as before. I'll just do more office and less floor."

"I'm not saying it's not a real job, don't get me wrong. It's just... life's easier with a diploma."

"I know, Mom."

"Assistant manager, but with a diploma."

"I promise."

"You can do what you want after college. Nobody says you hafta go on to university..."

The velvety word caressed her mouth.

"My daughter, the assistant manager. Can't hardly believe it..."

"Only of the dining room. I'm going to help with some of the paperwork."

"Still!"

"Yeah, still."

"You won't move out, will you?"

"No, Mom, come on. This won't change a thing, don't worry."

"Will you need new clothes, then? Some fancy pants, new shoes?"

"No, no, it's fine. I'm keeping the same uniform."

"You know your father's real proud of you, eh? It might not seem that way 'cause he's not a big talker, but I bet everyone down at the garage has heard all about it by now."

"I bet."

"You could drop by later for a quick hello, I'm sure he'd love it. He's just so proud of you..."

"Okay, I'll try."

"I put a book on your desk."

"I haven't finished the other ones yet. Plus, I have to read *Maria Chapdelaine* for French class."

"You already read it."

"Yeah, but that was so long ago I barely remember it."

"It doesn't end well, that's for sure. She picks the worst of the three. I'd 'a gone to the States."

Yeah right. My mother wouldn't have gone anywhere. In real life, her world extended only as far as Lac Saint-Jean, to the property a cousin let us use whenever we visited family in a pop-up camper. The unknown stretched beyond this limit like scorched earth.

"What're you reading now?"

"Bah, with this cold snap an' all . . ."

"Not *The Thorn Birds* again?"

"Bingo."

"Mom! But you know it by heart."

"It cheers me up."

"It ends even worse than *Maria*!"

Over at the garage, most of the guys were in the pit poking through the ailing bowels of various cars. As always, the walls were papered with edifying calendars depicting women-objects sprawled across improbably clean vehicles that had clearly never seen a winter. They served to remind anyone who cared to look that we were part of the animal kingdom, after all. Jingle was the first to spot my calves.

"Watch out, boys! Them's manager legs!"

"Hey, Jing. Is my dad around?"

His answer was drowned out by the screech of the food truck as it pulled up to the garage. Like rats scurrying off a sinking ship, the guys abandoned their posts to pounce on egg-salad sandwiches, barbecued peanuts, and cheese curds. They hastily wiped their hands on their greasy coveralls, then ate and licked their fingers without a thought to whatever else they might be ingesting. I imagined that the floors of their stomachs resembled the soles of their shoes. No doubt a mechanic's autopsy would reveal an interior splattered with oil, as if someone had butchered an octopus. I'd punctured the ink sac of one during a dissection in biology class, so I knew what I was talking about.

"He went to Pintendre for some calipers. Shouldn't be long now; I put a buck on forty-two minutes."

"Ah, too bad."

"Hang on there, missy." I heard a voice at my side. "Snack's on me, whatever ya want."

Pichette never missed a chance to be kind to me. It was a challenge to turn down his offers and invitations without offending him. He was too much like my father.

"Heck yeah, Laurie! We're celebratin' your promotion!"

"Relax; assistant manager of the dining room is basically the hostess."

"Your Pony didn't start this morning?"

"It always starts."

"Well, bring it in for a lil' oil change, ya hear?"

Note to self: don't ever hang out next to the garage pit. It was different when my father was around; his presence was like a protective shield around me. But being there alone always spelled trouble. A potential trap by its very nature, this hole was filled with mountains of junk that consumed everything and anyone in sight. Here, the metaphors skewed sleazy: headlights were a woman's eyes; bumpers, her breasts ("jacked up" if the guys had their way); the frame — which the guys offered to "tune up" with a twist here and a yank there — was code for their bodies. And an oil change? Well, that was the ultimate act of love. The vulgarity dripping from these crass images stripped them of all magic and sensuality.

Over the years, my father had freed himself from the pit by turning into a sourcer of parts, though he'd never said as much. His hands, tattooed with grease and mangled by a lifetime of minor injuries, were ravaged by arthritis, his fingers twisted in knotty, inhuman branches. He was missing half his right pinkie and the tip of his left index finger. He now spent most of his time running between auto dealers, other garages, and scrapyards he knew like the back of his hand. Whenever a part was hard to find, discontinued, or overpriced, he'd head to one of these metal graveyards with wire cutters and a crowbar and bend-twist-cut to extricate the precious object the dealer refused to sell as a single unit. For my father, matters of money and principle were intimately related. He was the Robin Hood of scrap metal. The guys would bet on how long it would take him to find a part, but the fact that he would find it was never in question.

"Can I make a call?"

"Gotta talk to your lover?"

"Gotta talk to work about my new schedule."

"S'ok, I'm not jealous."

A thin film of grime covered everything in the reception area, or "cockpit," that served as both store and dumping ground. The air was slick with grease and garbage juice, as if the entire room had been flooded in motor oil and very slowly drained. I searched everywhere but couldn't find a clean cloth I could use to lift the sticky receiver. I'd just extended my search to Ron's office when the door chimed.

"Hello!"

"Uh...hello."

"I'd like to fill up..."

"It's self-service."

"The problem is, I can't get my fuel door to open."

He was in his early twenties, with an understated, almost atypical beauty, hazel eyes, teeth too straight to be the product of genetics alone. I'd never seen him before. I glanced outside: black Golf GTI. Clearly not from around here. The guys were still milling around the food truck, warming their cheeks in the steam from their dishwater coffee, feet shuffling in the November slush.

"Uh...I don't really work here."

"Robbing the joint?"

"I wouldn't even want to, it's so dirty."

Dimple, left side. A wrinkle shaped like an integral symbol was stamped between his eyes. Hands hidden by the counter.

"I'll get one of the guys to come help you."

"Thanks."

He moved aside to let me pass, raising one finger to indicate that he'd tried to find a logical explanation for his problem.

"It might be frozen shut."

"Nah, it's not cold enough."

I went out and gently pressed on the fuel door to gauge its resistance, then gave it one swift smack with the side of my fist, so I wouldn't damage anything. The door popped open like I'd hoped.

"Wow!"

"The cable might have snapped."

"Can it be fixed?"

"Of course."

"My radio isn't working, either."

"What's the matter with it?"

"It can't find a signal."

"Does it crackle?"

"A little. It's weird."

"Jingle does all the electronics. I'll send him over. In the meantime, turn on your lights."

"My lights?"

"It's probably a loose contact."

In the natural light, a scattering of freckles had appeared on his face. I wanted to touch them, to feel his skin. His right ear stuck out just a bit. He was at least a head taller than me.

"JINGLE! THERE'S A GUY HERE WHO NEEDS YOUR HELP!"

I waved goodbye and went home to make my call. My mother was just leaving for work, and I caught her on her way out.

"Hey, Mom! Where's *Pride and Prejudice*?"

"Don't you know that one by heart?"

"Ha ha, very funny."

"In the hallway, third pile. What happened to *Maria*?"

"Ah, I remembered the story in the end. I just skimmed it."

"And?"

"And what?"

"Which guy would you have chosen?"

"Hmm... The one who gets lost in the woods, even if he's a damn fool."

As usual, on the flyleaf of *Pride and Prejudice*, my mother had pencilled in a number to keep her days organized: 9.

5

In some obscure corner of my mind, I pictured the big guns from Toronto to be much like the Terminator, so I fully expected him to share the cyborg's take-no-prisoners style. After all, he had been sent to the restaurant to trim the fat and turn around our profitability problem. But the dandy who strode into the dining room was nothing like the superhero I'd imagined. He was slim and elegant, and for his grand entrance he did a funny little grapevine dance before launching into a colourful presentation that fit his blue linen suit to a tee. If I'd been standing next to him, I'd have reached out to touch it. In his pocket, folded into a dapper pie-shaped triangle, a yellow silk handkerchief bobbed to the rhythm of his pale hands, accenting the words he'd chosen to assure us he'd been around the block before. He had saved some of ToRONto's best RESTaurants, and he fully intended to raise this one up to its rightful place, the place we all deserved to occupy — the *top*! The cooks, packed together like sardines in the back of the room, rolled their eyes and sighed in despair, as if they were being forced to watch an inspirational chick flick.

"But you have to believe! You have to *want* to be at the top!"

"Hooray."

"We'll start by getting a feel for the restaurant, defining its essence... really soaking it in, becoming one with it."

From the rising crescendo of grumbles and groans, it was clear that the idea of becoming one with the restaurant thrilled nobody.

"*Uno!* We're an Italian restaurant, so we need to channel Italy — taste it, feel it, *see* it. You're not in Vanier off Boulevard Hamel anymore. You're in Italy, in the old country, walking through a vineyard bathed in sunlight with the smell of tomatoes all around... We aren't selling food, we're selling an Italian experience.

"*Due!* Italians talk with their hands. If we want to bring Italy to life, we have to go the whole nine yards. If a customer asks whether a certain dish is good, you don't say 'Yeah, not bad,' with your hands stuffed in your apron. You make an O with your thumb, index, and middle fingers, bring it just under your nose, and give a good *delizioso!* You greet the customers with a *Buongiorno, signora!* and see them out with a *Buona notte, signore!"*

"Pff...Christ..."

"You, in the back. Do you have something to say, young man?"

"Nah, I'm good."

"No, please, I insist. We're on the edge of our chairs. What did you want to say?"

"This is a bunch of crap. Nobody here speaks Italian for real."

"And?"

"So nobody's gonna believe we speak Italian."

"Is that what you think?"

"Yeah."

"When people order a *napolitana* pizza...do you think they believe they're eating a Neapolitan-style pizza from Naples?"

"Uh...I dunno."

"When they order a *rigatoni pollo florentina* and have to point to the menu because they can't pronounce it, do you really think you're serving them an Italian dish?"

"Pff!"

"Do you think we serve authentic gelato here?"

"How should I know?"

"Of course not, my friend. We're not serving Italian dishes any more than you're speaking Italian. Any actual Italian who ate here would call our minestrone soup *bullshit.* And take the dining room! Do you think that's what an Italian kitchen really looks like? Do you think Italians decorate with trellises covered in plastic grapevines? That they use polyester tablecloths with big green olives printed on them? That they have stucco walls dotted with fake bricks? Of course not, it's *all* bullshit. But maybe it's my mistake — maybe I didn't explain it well enough the first time.

"Let me start over. Why do people want to eat here? Because they're looking for an Italian experience that matches the North American image they have of Italy. Our job isn't to rethink the image of the chain or the image people have in their minds. It's to improve it, spiff it up, fuel the illusion they're looking for, the illusion we're selling, so everyone is happy — especially you, since your paycheque depends on it. Remember, we're talking *illusion* and not authenticity. If all you can manage is a *bun journo* instead of a *buongiorno*, nobody's going to know the difference. As you pointed out, nobody here actually speaks Italian. And if we happen to come across some real Italians, they're going to think it's cute you're trying so hard and failing so spectacularly. That being said, I'm not forcing anybody here to play along or drink the Kool-Aid. You're free to go whenever you want. Capeesh?"

There followed a very long Italian–North American silence.

"*Tre!* From here on out, my name is Claudio. If you emphasize the *O*, it sounds fancier. It doesn't matter whether I look Italian or not. You, miss? What's your name?"

"Me? Uh...Diane."

"Diane...Diane...how about Dina?"

"Dina?"

"Pretty, isn't it?"

"Uh...yeah, sure."

"And you?"

"Me? Francine."

"Hmm. Francine can become...Francesca?"

"Oh! That's hard to say."

"We'll practice."

"Can I pick something else, even if it's not close?"

"Like what?"

"Well, if we're going with Italian, I'd rather be... Sophia."

"Sophia?"

"Yeah, like Loren."

"Sold! To Sophia."

"Thank you!"

"Lucky! I should have picked before you." There were a few whispers in the back.

"And you, behind her. My friend who seems annoyed. What's your name?"

"Me?"

"Yes, you."

"Jean-Seb."

"Short for Jean-Sébastien, I'd guess?"

"Yup."

"Jean-Sébastien...Jean-Sébastien...let's go with... Jean-Sébastien."

"For real?"

"Kitchen staff can keep their names, unless you'd like to play along."

"Call me Gino!"

With the exception of Charles, who thought it was "a fuckin' joke" and that Carlos or Fabio sounded "way too gay"—if he'd seen the Fabio of my mother's Harlequin novels, he might have changed his tune—everyone chose to stay and play Italian make-believe. Some took the role-playing further than others. Now that she was officially called Sophia, Francine went to great lengths to emulate the famous actress, using dyes, false eyelashes, and strategic padding to try to recreate some of the movie star's most striking assets. The guys in the kitchen relished calling attention to the older woman's transformation; under the guise of the game, Francine seemed to be satisfying a side of herself that had previously gone unfulfilled. Unsurprisingly, the new girl had slipped into the skin of Julia, the "pretty woman" of the hour, so the same kitchen guys spent their shifts asking how much she charged for a blow job. In fact, as everybody fell into their roles, they exposed flashes of personality usually reserved for Halloween. Dina began singing Dalida, Karina started ordering the staff around, hand on her hip, and Pablo grew a moustache that he twisted up at the ends à la Dalí (like just about everyone else, he thought the famous painter had been Italian). Out of respect for her age, nobody had asked Estelle to change her name. Instead of a noble Italian woman, *Estella* was more evocative of *Robin et Stella,* a children's TV show from the eighties, and the guys from the kitchen were all over that one.

My name was changed to Laura. The vowel switch required little more than opening the mouth a tad wider at the end of my real name. And since my mother had wanted to name me after Laura Ingalls, anyway, the new moniker brought me closer to my roots. Like with the other staff, this parallel life — in my case inspired by a single letter — had roused new desires in me: I began wearing burgundy lipstick, which I preferred to call *Valpolicella*. From a distance, it made me look like I had a big hole in the middle of my face.

Cindy hated my new name right away.

"I don't wanna call you that!"

"It's just pretend."

"I don't like pretenning!"

"It's just at the restaurant."

"No, ever'buddy's calling you that now!"

"They're just kidding."

"I don't like kidding!"

"They're just a bunch of kidders who like kidding around."

"Pff..."

"Big silly kidders kidding like big kids, I'm not even kidding."

"Pff... stop that, s'not funny."

"Oh no? Pee... poop... fart!"

"Pff... NO! STOPPIT!"

"Don't worry about it, bug. It's just a made-up name, like on TV."

"NO!"

"Stop shouting."

"NO NO NO NO NO! PLUS, NOW YOU WORK LATE ALL THE TIME! I HATE THE RESTAURANT!"

Sometimes she would wait for me all evening, circling the block and dragging her feet. And since I'd started going out for beers with the kitchen staff after weekend shifts — something Sonia didn't approve of, either — I'd often sleep in to find my days shortened at both ends. My mother tried her best to stand in for me, but Cindy had nowhere else to direct her ire. She'd had enough of my mother's stupid fruit that wasn't even good, wouldn't set foot inside her smelly house, refused to talk to the big, fat meanie. And to be absolutely certain my mother understood this, she stuck close to the apartment and kept her eyes glued to the door. The ones who stay always bear the brunt of things.

"Okay, calm down. I get it."

"Pff…"

"Should we go to the cabin?"

"…"

"You're still sulking, I see."

"Naw."

"I can't even tempt you with a hot chocolate by the fire?"

"Only if there's marshmallows."

"I'm not sure we have any left."

"But I want some!"

"Don't be rude, stop whining. We'll go buy more at the corner store if we're all out."

"Whatta 'bout a scary story?"

"Which one?"

"Baba Yaga!"

"That one's *too* scary."

"Not for me!"

The cabin was my mother's idea. We would sit around a space heater (the fireplace) in the living room, plunged in total darkness and snuggled up underneath my quilt, squeezed together like sardines to protect ourselves from the cold and the flies. Outside, a dense forest surrounded us, swarming with wolves, fireflies, and elves. No spiders, though. If you can choose, why not? Beyond the forest was a lake full of seahorses. Cindy thought trout, even rainbow trout, were too boring.

"I want five marshmallows."

"No, we said three. That's enough. They're big ones! You'll be sick otherwise."

"But I want mooore!"

"Baba Yaga loves gobbling up whiny little kids..."

I always picked the right moment to turn on the flashlight and shine it under my chin. If I made my spookiest face, I could almost scare her.

Just as we'd agreed before Carole left, I began drafting new plans to divide the restaurant dining room. I drew the room to scale to faithfully reproduce the current layout and new décor. I redistributed the sections according to the number of servers working, making sure to provide flexible options for the most popular tables, and superimposed these backup plans onto a system of overhead transparency sheets of my own design. This way, the coveted window booths—tables seventy-two through seventy-eight—could be reassigned throughout the evening depending on how busy the restaurant was at any given time. It was difficult to account for their popularity; my only theory was that the natural light made up for the desolate view of the parking lot.

My new system only worked if the sections were duly rotated. As assistant manager, that task fell to me. Since I'd carefully transferred the floorplans using Letraset, and Claudio had presented and backed them from the beginning, no one suspected me of being their architect. He asked that any criticism be addressed to him, and defended tooth and nail a system I wasn't even sure he supported. Of course, introducing a modicum of equity didn't please everyone; the most senior servers saw themselves stripped of previously unchallenged privileges. But the cheers of the rest of the servers, combined with the *ka-ching!* of money rolling in, had quickly buried all complaints that socialism was rearing its ugly head.

Meanwhile, customers were delighted with the restaurant's Italian makeover and enchanted by the attentions of its new boss. Claudio took it upon himself to greet them, to make sure everything was to their liking, and to offer each client their moment in the sun. These came in the form of a compliment for the women and a virility boost for the men: the *madames* always wore clothes that flattered their figures and hairstyles that made them look younger; the *monsieurs* were generous husbands and fathers who knew how to live well and pamper their loved ones. Claudio had a phenomenal memory and kept track of even the smallest personal details. The little tidbits he so skillfully gathered allowed him to treat complete strangers like friends, a technique that was particularly appealing to people who led humdrum little lives. It wasn't uncommon to see customers-turned-friends reverse course whenever— alas!—Claudio took a day off, winking and making allusions to their closeness as they retreated.

"You tell him that Pete the Zamboni came by tonight. Just tell him, he'll understand. I'll drop by tomorrow. He'll be here, won't he?"

"Absolutely."

"Tell him, you'll see. He'll understand right away."

"*Sì, Signore. Buona notte.*"

Often, at the end of the night, once I'd finished all the paperwork and tweaked the following day's schedule in light of unforeseen circumstances, Claudio would come into the office to look over the day's numbers. He scrupulously noted the glasses of white wine he drank in the Promos book and let me touch the fabric of his shirts. Around the third glass, he'd often switch to English. Camouflaged by the accent of an adopted language that inspired trust, he would tell me things he believed to be secret, unspeakable truths.

"You have to know, Laura, that I'm...I'm..."

"I know."

"Really? You really know?"

"Everybody knows, Claudio. I don't see how it changes anything."

"For you, it doesn't. But it's probably best not to tell the big boss."

"Are you serious?"

"Welcome to the Middle Ages, darling."

"Is your shirt silk?"

"Not the real deal, honey."

Claudio's constant presence in both the dining room and kitchen soon led him to discover that the ship was leaking from all sides. Keeping a close watch on inventory revealed that every month we were mysteriously losing a good twenty litres of Bolognese sauce, five or six boxes of vegetables, a few kilos of pasta (mainly cannelloni), more than a few sausage links, and a great deal of other pseudo-Italian meat products. In the dining room, nearly ten litres of house wine disappeared altogether, and the bottles of liquor seemed to have holes in the bottom, a problem the electronic pour spouts never seemed to help. Inventory also revealed that although we went through desserts quickly, we sold relatively few. Everyone tried to explain away these losses with the old adage that restaurants had to lose money to make money, it was all well and good. When you tallied up everything that was ruined, dropped, burned, mixed up, or forgotten, nearly all the numbers could be accounted for. Based on this logic, the questions began to change:

it was no longer about where the wine went, but whether we were careful enough pouring it. We tried to determine which servers, given to excesses of generosity, cut six slices from a cake meant to serve eight. Oddly enough, as soon as they were uncovered, these irregularities tapered off until they almost stopped, as if their mere discovery had been enough to adjust the numbers to reality.

In the following weeks, however, old habits slipped back into the machinery of daily life. Claudio kept a watchful eye out, always lurking in the shadows. He never stepped in. Instead, he took the time to study the problem and collect evidence. He didn't miss a single delivery and always helped carry the boxes to the walk-ins. His eyes were everywhere and saw everything: the desserts we "forgot" to charge for, the service doors we frequently opened to "air out the place" or smoke a cigarette. He was considerate enough to keep me out of his investigations, careful to withhold any information that might have put me in an awkward position with the others. He'd ask me for this or that—a sales report, someone's schedule, a pay slip, a purchase order— always wrapped in a please-and-thank-you, always with a smile to mask the fact that this witch hunt was, in fact, killing him.

One by one, the offenders were called into Claudio's office for a little tête-à-tête. Some were in and out in minutes, while others stayed for hours. Dina cried, Luc punched the wall, J.P. kicked a few chairs across the staff room, and Floria — whose real name was Blanche — took me for a confidante as she handed me her apron.

"I had no choice. I'm suing my ex to keep him from seeing my daughter, and the goddamn lawyers are bleeding me dry."

"I don't know anything. I just take care of the paperwork."

"I didn't punch in the coffees. What's a bag of beans cost them? They're over here getting rich off coffee they steal from poor folks, and they call *me* a thief? They deserve what they get."

" . . . "

"Jerks like that can't handle getting jerked around, simple as that."

"I guess."

"I'll find something else. I always do."

"'Course you will."

"Bye, Laura. You're a nice girl. Stay in school, okay?"

Head held high, Claudio played the role of executioner until the door closed. Then his head would drop under the weight of the pain he'd inflicted on others. His chin fell on his chest like a dagger. He hated himself. And he chased away the storm clouds with gulps of white wine.

In the chaos of the shake-up, I let a handful of serving positions pass me by. But I wasn't worried. My time would come. For now, Claudio needed me.

6

"Shit! MOM!"

"WHAT?"

"I'VE GOT LICE! I CAN SEE THEM JUMPING AROUND!"

Out of nowhere, a tiny creature had landed on the diagram of an electrical circuit I was copying for physics class. I crushed it with my thumbnail, smearing a little dot of blood on the paper where the light bulb should have been.

"Can't be! We used the special shampoo and washed everything twice!"

"That dirty little brat!"

"It's not her fault."

"No, it's those idiot parents who aren't doing their

job! I'm gonna kill 'em!"

"Don't say things like that. Do they itch?"

"No, they jump!"

"Show me. Hmm...yeah...Oh, I see...okay... Right, of course."

"I have to work at four! I'll never be able to go like this!"

"Stay here, I'll run to the drugstore. Make a little turban out of an old towel so they can't escape."

"But their crappy shampoo doesn't even work!"

"We'll leave it in longer this time, maybe we didn't wait long enough. I'll stop by the Sunoco on the way back to let Cindy's dad know."

"That dickhead won't give a shit!"

"Don't swear like that. I'll be back in a jiffy, don't move."

The pharmacist had nothing to suggest but the usual shampoo, grown powerless against these mutant lice (the same problem faced by farmers who used pesticides, as I'd learned in biology class). But the girls at the makeup counter, summoned by the sounds of my mother's distress, sang the praises of an unbeatable solution.

"A hair dye?" I was sceptical.

"Baby, they said it's so strong it kills near everything. And the critters won't come back, either. Something about not being able to stick to the hair afterwards."

"What's that mean?"

"The girls said it really does a number on the hair sheath, makes it turn slippery or something. I'll have to ask Louise how it works."

"They might be right, Mom. You dye your hair, and you never get lice!"

"I don't have the head for it. I never got lice, even when I was little. Everyone around me had 'em, but not me."

"Guys are lucky, they can just shave their heads."

"For your length, the girls think it'll probably take two boxes."

"Buy ten if you have to, as long as it works."

"Pick your colour, and I'll go back."

"What did Cindy's dad say?"

"Said she's never had lice in her life."

"What an idiot."

"I gave him a box of the shampoo just the same. I told 'im what to do, but he might not know how to read."

The girls at the drugstore had been thoughtful enough to loan me the ring of Nice'n Easy colour samples so I could choose without leaving the house. I spent the next half hour posing in front of the mirror, holding the various shades to my temples to judge their effect on my eyes. I called Sonia for her opinion.

"RED! Do red, it's soooo pretty!"

"But that'll be too obvious!"

"Isn't that the idea? You're dyeing it, so you might as well change things up."

"I was thinking about dark brown. It's close to my natural colour."

"Ugh, no! Stop being so uptight. Go with a nice blond and get rid of that stupid ponytail!"

"*Blond*-blond?"

"Yes, blond-blond. An ash blond."

Once my mother had washed away the brownish, beery lather, the colour appeared in all its horror. It was a far cry from the ash blond that lit up the face of the girl on the box.

"Don't panic, we have to dry it first. You can never tell what the real colour'll be when it's wet."

"It's yellow. YELLOW! I can't go out looking like this."

"It's not *that* yellow. You're just not used to it."

"It's piss yellow, like when you've been holding it in for a while."

Louise agreed to see us, even though the salon was closed. My mother had fed her a little speech peppered with threats to my wellbeing, including phrases like "future in jeopardy," "psychological distress," and "dark thoughts."

"Drugstore dye? Don't tell me she used that crap. You gotta bleach it to get blond, everyone knows that! Well, not you, Suzanne, not with that auburn. But at least it killed the lice, or I wouldn't've let you through the door. Lice at a hairdresser's — can you imagine? Just leave it to Loulou, I'll get you all cleaned up."

We drove the three blocks to the basement apartment Louise shared with her seven cats, part of which served as an undercover salon. Two hours later, and fully convinced she must have mixed car battery-acid into her colour, I walked out permanently de-loused — or so I hoped, at least — as an almost-natural ash blonde. My hair was cut blunt just below my shoulders (the last foot hadn't survived the bleach's spectacularly corrosive wash). The moment I saw Louise eagerly plugging in her curling iron, I feared I would end up with Nellie Oleson's tight ringlets, so I declined the style. I didn't have time, anyway. I had a restaurant to get to. Outside, an icy breeze was waiting to nip at my raw scalp.

"Leave it down! How pretty are you, eh, Suzanne? Isn't she pretty?"

"I can't get over it... Your father's gonna love it! Always did have a thing for blondes."

"Were you ever a blonde, Mom?"

"Oh gosh, no! I never had the face for it."

"What does that mean?"

"You need a pretty face to be a blonde, or it doesn't work. And you're such a pretty girl..."

"Mom..."

Once I arrived at the restaurant, a mere hour late, I fielded more compliments than Scarlett O'Hara strolling across the green fields of Georgia. Estelle teared up when she saw how my head was "glitterin' alluva sudden." The guys took turns whistling at me from the receiving line they'd formed between the kitchen and staff room entrances. I was flattered, but still told them off on principle. Standing before the broken mirror of the women's bathroom, I studied the kaleidoscope of my face from every angle. Estelle was right about the glitter. It worked. The fluorescent bulb cast a shimmery rectangle onto the side of my head. It made me look like a manga character. I reapplied the Valpolicella lipstick and lifted my chin, like a girl who is used to getting noticed.

After the shift, I went downtown with everybody else. Screw my biology exam—I'd do some last-minute cramming and spit it back out onto my paper before I forgot it all for good. My hair wanted to sway back and forth on a dance floor, adding its fire to the twinkle of a gigantic disco ball. And I didn't disappoint. I danced better with my new hair. I practically floated. The other dancers tossed me looks that got caught in my golden nets. I felt pretty. I *was* pretty.

When I saw him, my whole body was pulsing to the vibrations from the speaker I was standing on. One hand on his hip and the other gripping the neck of a beer, he was smiling up at me from the foot of my stela with his head cocked slightly back for a better view. He'd recognized me; I was surprised. Even in this bar, the air thick from the heat of a thousand sweaty dancers, the collar of his polo shirt refused to bend. With an index finger, he pointed to his (beautiful) head of hair, frowning.

"YOUR HAIR?"

"WASN'T MY CHOICE!"

We could scarcely hear each other, even when we shouted at the tops of our lungs.

"I HAD LICE!"

"WHAT?"

"LICE!"

Other than Sonia, I hadn't told anyone why I'd dyed my hair. Oddly enough, the truth seemed less embarrassing than saying that I'd become a blonde by choice. I surprised even myself.

"I HAD LICE, BUT NOW THEY'RE GONE!"

"LICE ARE AFRAID OF BLONDES?"

"HAH!"

I reached out for him to help me down and let my hand linger a few seconds on his baby-soft skin, satiny palms, and smooth knuckles on undamaged fingers.

His smile widened—he found all this amusing. Drained by alcohol and fatigue, I felt a sudden need to sit down, anywhere. I put my hand on his shoulder to steady myself. If he had offered to pick me up and part the crowd to take me outside, like in the movies, I'd have let him.

"Thanks for that thing the other day."

"WHAT THING?"

"THE THING FOR THE RADIO!"

"OH!"

"IT DOES THE TRICK. UNTIL THE PARTS COME IN."

From behind me, Jean-Sébastien appeared, smelling of Alfredo sauce. I felt his over-proteined pecs rub up against my back.

"YOU OKAY, LAU?"

His mouth was three inches from my ear, but he was shouting loud enough for everyone around us to hear. I stuck out my tongue before I turned around.

"I'm okay."

"YOU SURE THIS PANSY-ASS ISN'T BOTHERING YOU?"

"Of course not, he's a friend. I'm fine." Then, to get rid of Jean-Seb, I said, "Go back to Julie."

It never failed: after a few beers, Jean-Sébastien was always looking to "take care of" the girls, even if it meant causing trouble. And since I'd made the mistake of kissing him once— okay, twice—he felt duty bound to protect me. He wasn't a bad guy, but I liked him better bent over the stove, when the pizza rushes channelled his excess testosterone and hid the fact that some of his bolts weren't screwed on tightly enough.

"WHAT'S YOUR NAME?"

"LAU-RIE. YOURS?"

"RO-MAN."

"ROMAN?"

"YUP!"

He raised his white hand as if to say, "Not my fault!" Of course. He couldn't have been a Kevin or a Steve. Guys like him are classy all the way down to their birth certificates. He was my first Roman, not counting the legionnaires who got beaten to a pulp in *Asterix*. Someone I'd never seen before, presumably a friend of his, materialized next to him to bellow something, using his hands as a megaphone. Roman shook his head no. The guy turned to me and smiled, as if to say, "It's all good, I got it." He gave Roman a manly slap on the shoulder and walked off.

"ARE YOU HUNGRY?"

"HUNGRY?"

"YEAH, LIKE FOR A POUTINE."

My mother had used the iron to make me a grilled cheese, and I'd eaten it in the car before my shift. It was now the wee hours of the morning, and I was hungry enough to eat two horses.

"WHERE WERE YOU THINKING?"

"ASHTON?"

"LEMME SAY BYE, I'LL BE RIGHT BACK!"

Of course, Jean-Seb clenched his fists when I told him I was going to grab a bite with my "friend." He didn't like the idea of me leaving with any guy, friend or not, pansy-ass or not. If he'd known I was hungry, he would have whipped up a J.S. special at the end of our shift.

"YOU CAN MAKE ME ONE TOMORROW."

"IT WOULDA BEEN BETTER THAN SOME CRAPPY POUTINE."

"I KNOW. YOU'RE SO SWEET. TAKE CARE OF JULIA TONIGHT!"

He made the sign of the devil's horns and stuck out his tongue. I felt sorry for any poor guy who dared approach *his* pretty woman.

After elbowing and tripping our way through the crowd to get our coats, Roman offered me a navy jacketed arm so that, together, we could find a path to the exit. When I recounted the scene to Sonia the following day, I wasn't able to do it justice. She couldn't picture our departure resembling anything out of a musical. I guess you had to be there.

The frigid air took our breath away the moment our bodies cut through the wall of cold outside. We exhaled deceptive puffs of air that looked like smoke. Our clothes reeked of cigarettes to their very fibres.

"Listen to the snow crunch, it must be twenty below." Now that I had less hair, the cold felt crueller.

"It's the perfect temperature."

"Hah! Why perfect?"

"Because ticks die at twenty below."

"Ticks? You mean those gross little bugs?"

"Yeah, the ones that suck animal blood."

"The ones that go in head-first?"

"Yeah. They're like ostriches, but on your body..."

"Ew, Roman!"

"Lots of other bugs die at twenty below. I love the cold. It's so useful!"

"Are you a bug specialist?"

"Indirectly."

"Car batteries die in the cold, too. That's not as cool."

"Are you a car battery specialist?"

"Indirectly."

Behind us, a pack of staggering drunk guys tried to beat us to the entrance of Ashton. Their shouts mingled together to form a bristly mash of "HEY, YO"s and slurred obscenities, "FUUUKKIT." To shut them up, Jean-Seb would have skewered them; Roman just smiled at them. One guy who hadn't managed to overtake us stood a few feet back, mumbling flat beer burps into his unmittened hands. Roman slowed his pace.

"Go ahead, you can pass us."

"NAAAW! MMMNOT INNA RUSH."

He was gritting his teeth; we should have known better. Suddenly his body, then his throat, rose in one great swell like a garden hose rearing from the water pressure and he spewed vomit all over the sidewalk. For the subsequent waves he was down on all fours, palms in the road salt. He retched long after his stomach had anything to expel.

Roman dodged the tail end of the first jet like a bullfighter, but I'd already taken the brunt of it. The brownish mess splashed across my coat in a perfect diagonal, from my left shoulder down to my right thigh. The drunk friends circled back as Roman took his scarf, wrapped it around a gloved fist, and tried to wipe off the gelatinous muck the cold was already crystallizing onto my coat.

"Stop it, you'll ruin your scarf."

"I can wash it."

"HEYY! SORRY, MAN! SORRY 'BOUT HIM... HE'S A GOOD KID, JUST GOIN' THROUGH SOME ROUGH STUFF..."

"It's fine. No big deal. Don't leave him in the snow like that, he'll get frostbite."

"BUT HE'S GONNA PUKE SUMMORE..."

They were big, snot-nosed children, soft all over.

"Go in and take him to the bathroom! Call him a cab! Don't leave him there! I doubt he's got much left to puke up, anyway."

While their neurons slowly fired up, Roman dragged their sick friend into the restaurant. I stood in the bitter cold under the streetlight, watching the swirls of powdery snow illuminate the Saint-Louis Gate in the distance. I'd lost my appetite, anyway, and there wasn't a restaurant in town that would let me in smelling the way I did. The first cab I hailed pulled over; I was amazed by the power of blond hair. Roman came running back. He wanted me to go to his place. We could get cleaned up, rescue our appetite, talk about bugs, cars, whatever.

"I can't, I feel so gross."

"I live five minutes away."

"I don't even know you."

"Roman Leduc, twenty-one, five-nine-and-a-half, O positive. I have three cavities and recently got my tetanus booster. Fructose intolerant, favourite colour indigo, Zodiac sign... banana."

"Pff! Do you go to university?"

"When I remember to."

The taxi honked.

"I can't, but want to spend your five minutes where it's warm?"

"No, thanks. I might never want to get out..."

I took off my coat and rolled it into a ball, nauseating splatters of barf on the inside like a stuffed turkey, and ducked into the passenger seat of the overheated cab. I wanted to at least spare the driver. Roman drummed

It was around eleven by the time I cracked open my eyes, pulled from sleep by a quiet babbling. *Brrr, pit-pit-pit, shhhhh, pli, pla, pli, pla*... Through the slit in my eyelids — impossible to detect from the outside, my lashes were still thick with mascara — I watched Cindy play games with her hands. She was on her back, legs bent above her, twirling her fingers in the dusty sunbeam that sliced through the room. They danced in the air to a complex choreography of her own creation, climbing endless stairs and twisting into abstract shapes. Scattered all around her in a jumbled little nest were the books and crayons my mother had brought to keep her quiet. She was waiting for me. My bedroom had always been her favourite place. I was her best, her only friend. In the shadow of my sleep, which everyone protected like a holy relic, she spent hours in a state of active boredom that fostered patience. Similar to a kitten, she had a habit of falling asleep as she played, hands in midair.

"Hey there, kid."

"Geez, you been sleepin' all day!"

I lifted up the quilt, giving her the go-ahead to jump into bed with me.

"Shit! What happened to your hair?"

She wrapped her skinny arms around her head.

"Nuffin.'"

"My God! Show me . . . move your arms."

"Nooo. Leamme alone."

"You can't stay like that all day. I'll see it sooner or later, so you might as well just show me now."

"Nooo!"

"Did you cut it?"

"Not me."

"Then who?"

"My ma did."

"Your mom? Because of the lice?"

"I DON'T HAVE LICE! IT'S THE STUPID GIRLS AT SCHOOL WHO DO!"

My mother poked her head through the door.

"Goodness, what's going on here? I thought you two were sleeping!"

"Mom, did you see her hair?"

"'Course I did, honey."

"It looks awful!"

"It's not so bad. Her mom did the special shampoo an' fixed her up with a home cut."

She'd been butchered—there was no other word to describe the carnage. Bangs had been inelegantly shorn two inches from the roots, "to last longer." Between the skinny arms covered in scratches and bruises she was holding up to hide her head, little tufts of hair poked out, as if they'd been ripped and not cut. She looked like a massacred doll, the kind you throw away because it's too scary. I held back an urge to scream.

"The lice're all gone, I just looked her over."

"Would it have killed the woman to take her to the salon? Crazy bi—"

"Laurie! Come on, girls, I made French toast."

"Yuck! I don't eat French stuff!"

"Well, come anyway, there's kiwi. And you do like French toast, you just forget half the time. Plus, mine always tastes different, depends on what's in my fridge."

"Why'd you change your hair, Laulau?"

I'd almost forgotten. In my head, I started scrolling through the images of the day before, starting with the cheap dye and ending with the taxi, with everything in between.

"Because I wanted to."

"I don't like it."

"Well, you don't like anything, so you don't count."

My mother and I had come to believe we could provide Cindy with at least part of what her parents weren't. We'd catch her in mid-flight and do our best to fatten her up a little before releasing her back into the wild. It did us as much good as it did her. But her ravaged head was a violent reminder of the absolute power they held over her, along with our utter power-lessness to make any real impact. I probably should just have gone back to bed. Instead, I dressed in a hurry, threw on my mother's coat — mine was making its third trip through the wash — and dashed out.

I ran blindly through alleys and down streets, past the cracked asphalt in front of Cindy's house, up the spiral staircase, across the morass of her balcony, and didn't stop until I hit the slovenly kitchen. In a living room so hazy it felt like a bar, a woman in a bathrobe was rolling cigarettes on a coffee table, eyes glued to a TV, where a greenish figure was mixing mayonnaise of the same shade. She was ageless: an old, worn-out young woman with lifeless eyes, neglected teeth, and a raspy voice. Rollers hung loosely from her head, as if her hair knew it wouldn't be going anywhere soon. Her spineless husband was nowhere in sight.

"Who're you?"

"You could've taken her to get a real haircut."

"Who the hell're you?"

"Laurie. Laulau. Cindy's friend."

A mountain of clothes was heaped on a threadbare carpet flecked with reddish burn marks. In one corner sat boxes of cassette tapes, their contents spilling out everywhere.

"Ah, so it's you. Not what I'd imagined."

"A haircut costs two packs of cigarettes."

"The kid's too antsy. She won't sit still long enough to get it cut. You all gimme shit when she comes home with lice, and you gimme shit when I take care of it!"

"If that's what you call taking care of it..."

"It's none of your goddamn business! I got every right to do what I want!"

"Crazy bitches like you just shouldn't be allowed to have kids."

"Get the fuck out of here, or I'll call the cops."

"THE COPS? GO AHEAD, CALL 'EM! I'LL TELL 'EM HOW YOU TREAT YOUR DAUGHTER! I'LL TELL 'EM HOW YOU CHUCK HER DOWN HOT DOGS FROM THE THIRD FLOOR, THAT THAT'S HOW YOU FEED HER. LIKE A DOG! LIKE A FUCKIN' DOG!"

"GET OUT, YOU LITTLE SHIT! GET! OUT!"

I felt a pair of powerful arms grab me from behind and I thought for a moment it was already the police. I threw my head back. Bad reflex.

"IT'S ME, FOR THE LUVVA GOD! It's just me... calm down."

My father and his quiet strength. A grip like a vise.

"OUT! OUT! GET THE HELL OUT, YOU ANIMALS!"

"YOU'RE THE ANIMAL, YOU JACKASS!"

"LAUR! Calm down! You've got no right to be here."

"I CAN GET YOU ARRESTED FOR TRESPASSING!"

"SHUT YOUR GODDAMN MOUTH! I CAN GET YOU ARRESTED FOR NEGLECT!"

My father loosened his grip once we were on the balcony. I spat out the bile that had risen in my throat. I was hopping like a madwoman.

"Cool your jets, the kid's watchin' us from down below."

There she was at the foot of the stairs, skinny arms hanging limply in her cheap coat, dark circles around eyes that stared, unseeing, into the gaping hole I'd just torn in the fabric of her life. Our two worlds could coexist as long as our paths ran parallel. They could bend and twist all they wanted, just as long as they never intersected. But by deviating from my own path, I had broken the rules and shattered the delicate balance that allowed us to be together.

"Cindy I just wanted to talk to your mother..."

"CINDY! GET UP HERE! MOVE IT!"

My father placed a hand on my arm and lowered his gaze. Cindy started up the stairs like a zombie.

"Don't say a thing, Lau. Not a word."

"Want to come back to our place later, kiddo?"

"CINDY! GET UP HERE THIS MINUTE! AND I DON'T WANNA SEE YOU TALKIN' TO HER!"

I was begging now. My voice trembled as I tried to inject a note of sweetness. I'd have given anything to go back in time and stop myself from running over here. But I knew it was no use. *Stay with me, baby sister, my little stray angel. Stay with me.*

"Maybe tomorrow? Hey, Cindy? Tomorrow? I'll be waiting..."

She ignored me as she passed, a fleeting soul sucked upstairs by the voice above.

"Let her go, Laurie. If we don't go now, we'll be in a heap a' trouble."

Down in the back alley, I kicked everything in my path — trash cans, ripped-out car seats, old bike frames twisted beyond repair, whatever the snow hadn't covered yet. My father followed calmly behind with his hands in his pockets, not trying to stop me. He'd seen me do this before and knew I'd run out of steam soon enough.

"Don't worry, Lau. It'll all be fine."

"No, it won't! She'll never come see us again! They're jackasses, both of them! Jackasses living in a goddamn shithole!"

"Oh yes, she will. She'll be back..."

"No, she hates me! SHE HATES ME!"

"Kids never hate for long. That stuff's only for adults. Even for stupid little things. Especially for stupid things…"

"She's not a normal kid."

"That's what you think."

"Dammit!"

"Come on, let's get your car."

"Shit! My car…"

"Left it at work?"

"Yeah."

"Parked by the river?"

"Yeah, behind the restaurant. Same as always."

"Better get going, then."

Overnight, blown by strong winds, a thin layer of powder had slipped under the hood of my car. The Pony coughed but refused to ignite the air-fuel mixture and fire up its four cylinders, despite my silent pleas. The wiring had gotten wet and the electrical system was feeling uncooperative.

"You shouldn't park facing the river. The wind off the water'll blow the snow under the hood and flood your spark plugs. We'll hafta grease 'em up a bit, just until we can change 'em."

"Did you bring some?"

WD-40 was my father's magic cure-all. Like a

SOME MAINTENANCE REQUIRED

grandpa and his handkerchief, he never went anywhere without it. It was impossible to count the many little problems it fixed in an instant; to this day, I haven't found a better stain remover. Once the spark plugs were lubricated, the Pony began to purr. Black slush started dropping from the mud guard in big clumps.

"We'll stop by the garage first, the guys are workin' on Ron's brakes. Gotta get her wiring up to snuff."

The garage owner let the guys open on weekends for personal repairs, as long as they paid for their own parts. After working for less accommodating bosses, they knew how lucky they were and wanted to hold on to their privileges, so they scrupulously noted the parts they used down to the smallest screw. It was an unwritten rule that nobody dared break. On the service bay doors, CLOSED signs fluttered in the breeze to discourage peepers and the occasional desperate soul searching for a garage open on a Sunday. The beer flowed like water and the atmosphere was as jolly as a churchyard after mass.

"Holy Christ! Marilyn's not dead after all!"

"Pheeew!"

"Well, looky who showed up!"

My mood was as black as old motor oil; I should have hightailed it home.

"It snowed in the car."

"What'd ya do, leave her titties wavin' in the breeze?"

The floodgates of blond jokes, pleasant as a hail-storm in summer, were about to burst open. The nude calendar pinned to the wall above the large Mastercraft tool chest showed a woman sprawled across the hood of a shiny new sports car. Her moonish breasts defied gravity in a feat that would have astounded my physics teacher. I wondered how a girl, or anyone, really, could get to that point, could experience such a fall from grace. What humiliations had she endured before accepting a job straddling cold, hard metal while freezing her ass off? What distant prospects had given her the strength to smile? And all that to spruce up the grimy walls of a garage somewhere.

"What'd the blonde say when they asked if her blinker worked? Nobody? It works, it don't work, it works, it don't work, it works... hah!"

"Wait, wait... Know why blondes need triangular coffins?"

"Nah."

"'Cause the second you lay one down, they spread their legs!"

I marched over to the calendar, to all those poor girls crucified on the wall, and tore it down. Month by month, I ripped the glossy paper depicting their asses, boobs, and mouths into pieces so small you'd never be able to tell what they'd once been. Then I tossed it like confetti around the garage and into the pit, so they'd be forced to walk across the scraps for weeks.

"For fuck's sake, you're crazy! What's gotten into you?"

"I'll tell ya what hasn't, that's for sure..."

I flashed him February, the sole image that had been spared.

"This girl's name is not Rosalita, and it's not her life goal to be fucked on the hood of a car."

"We ain't hurtin' nobody, it's just a picture."

"NO! IT'S NOT JUST A PICTURE! IT'S NOT JUST A FUCKING PICTURE! THAT'S WHAT ALL YOU DIPSHITS JACKING OFF TO THESE CALENDARS DON'T REALIZE! PULL YOUR HEADS OUT OF YOUR ASSES!"

On the ground, tattered bits of the girls' diaphanous skin were absorbed into the grime of garage life and slowly faded into the darkness. I slammed Rosalita down on the trunk, giving her an extra smack with the flat of my hand.

"Christ, Laulau..."

I didn't even have the strength to apologize. My father would smooth things over with them. Nobody said another word. They didn't have to—it was obvious I'd been having a tough time. These guys kept their troubles at bay by tending to car guts. We all do what we can.

• • •

My mother wasn't having much luck reading. A big pile of books, their spines perfectly stacked, took up half of the kitchen table. Her eyes skimmed the text but refused to settle on the words. Even as a kid, I could tell when she was anxious by the way she read. She would flip pages in both directions, forwards and backwards, stare at the title page, and sit with one finger glued to a spot that served less as a place marker than a lightning rod, keeping her grounded.

At the dinner table, gathered around plates heaped with meatballs fried in butter and topped with peas swimming in gravy, we tried to pretend everything was fine. In front of me, a mashed potato volcano held back the brown lava that was just a spoonful away from spilling out and flooding the plate. When I was small, I would add Playmobil men with swords and quivers of arrows, a glass of wine, a bouquet of flowers. Across from me, my father held his fork in one hand like a hammer, a beer in the other, and chewed with his mouth half open so it would taste better. The faded wallpaper behind him was curling at the seams. My mother had served my food on my favourite plate, the oval gold-rimmed one from Notre-Dame Hospital. She'd even let me use the Air Canada fork with the impossible-to-bend tines. And since I was having such a terrible day, I'd get to eat dessert with the spoon we'd bought at a church rummage sale organized by the Society of St. Vincent de Paul. It had saved me from the worst colds and stomach bugs, even a bout with scarlet fever. I would get over this, too.

Despite it all, the words I was struggling to suppress rose like a surprise burp, finding their way to the edges of my soul: "They have her living in that . . . goddamn shithole."

Cindy was back a few days later, hopping two-footed up each step of the wrought-iron staircase — a stunt that meant she at least had boots in her size. My mother stood up, hand flying to her heart as if it were Kateri Tekakwitha in the flesh, Doctor Zhivago settling in the dust at her feet. The girl's toque was pulled down tightly over her head, making it impossible to see anything but her mouth, twisted into an upside-down smile, as she walked in. Her chin was trembling, whether from cold or heartache it was hard to say.

"Hey there, kid!"

"Not hi."

She was vaguely angry with me, but the earful I'd been expecting never came. Once freed from underneath the hat, her eyes, brimming with distress, turned towards me. She was on the verge of tears.

"Hey now, sunshine. What's going on?"

"Everyone's laffin' at me . . ."

"Everyone who?"

"At school."

"Why's that?"

She pulled the toque off, revealing a shock of short hair, standing on end as if electrified. I thought it looked worse than before, though I tried to cover up my reaction with a gentle smile.

"It doesn't look that bad."

"But they're all laffin' at me!"

"It's an unusual look, I guess . . ."

My mother hastened to offer her peanut squares, juicy grapes, little pancakes in syrup. Cindy sat down and ate the snacks without taking off her coat or boots. Orders from home, no doubt. She probably wasn't allowed at our house anymore.

"Laurie and me, we know a lady who can fix hair."

"I don't buhleev you."

"I swear. The lady works magic. She could even up the ends on this side and soften it back here. It's a little too . . . square."

"What's she called?"

"Louise. But we call her Lulu."

"Sounds like Laulau."

"You'd be so pretty."

"But I don't wanna get it cut!"

"She won't cut it, she'll fix it, love. There's a difference."

"What about my mom?"

"Your mom'll be happy the kids at school aren't laughing at you anymore."

I'd never heard my mother dodge a question with so much aplomb.

Cindy sat in the middle of a chair that could have fit three of her, back straight, slightly afraid. She'd refused to take off her coat and get her hair washed. Louise had used a spray bottle to wet it, then subtly began tackling the uneven ends.

"I don't wanna cut it."

"Of course not, sweetie. I'm just fixin' it up a little, trust me. Lulu's gonna give you some nice layers."

"Wassat?"

"It's a way of cutting the hair so that when you run your hand through it, it sort of fans out like the wings of a bird. You'll see . . ."

I swept the cut bits into a little nest in the middle of my palm so that she wouldn't panic. In theory, we weren't cutting it.

"It looks like you're cutting."

"Those are just the ends, they don't count. For the hair to be nice and soft, you gotta get rid of the dry part. It's not real cutting, don't worry."

Once the operation was over and she saw her reflection in the big mirror framed with light bulbs, Cindy decided to approve of the layers. Her bony little fingers raked through the sides to see the wings fan out on her head.

"Want to go for a drive to show off your pretty hair?"

"Show it to who?"

"We could go..."

"See Sonia!"

"Okay, let's start with Sonia. And then... hmm... the bakery?"

"Stoopid."

"No way, you love the bakery! Those nice ladies always give you cookies!"

"Those fatties."

"Don't say that, it's not nice."

"I wanna frog cookie."

"Don't demand, it isn't polite."

As expected, her parents didn't notice a thing. If we were careful, we'd be able to keep existing in parallel worlds. I'd take what I could get.

8

By spring, the Pony was showing signs of wear. One
after another, its parts gave out like overripe fruit. But no
matter how much I tinkered with it — my muffler lasted
three extra weeks thanks to a jerry-rigged clamp — the
car always ended up back in the garage. My father, eyes
downcast, was crestfallen to see just how right he had
been. Cars were expensive.

The latch in the driver's side door gave up the ghost
as well. If the Pony were suddenly to burst into flames,
a scenario that was seeming less improbable by the day, I
would have to smash a window to escape. Since I didn't
want my father to lose another fingertip dismantling a
door in the middle of winter (the worst injuries happen
when fingers are numb from the cold), I would just

open the passenger door, put my bags down on the floor and slide over to the driver's side in one fluid motion as if it were the most natural thing in the world. I had the move down pat, so smooth my father still didn't suspect a thing. I now only gave rides to close friends who could see the humour in the situation. And of course, Cindy didn't see anything unusual about me doing a few gymnastics to get in and out of the car. After all, we travelled to Mexico on bath towels.

One morning, as I was getting ready to contort myself into the Pony for the sake of my chemistry class, Claudio pulled up alongside me.

"Morning, Laurie!"

There was no good reason a maximizer of profits from Toronto would be in this area. And certainly not at 7:30 on a Tuesday morning. I glanced around, hoping to understand. A big mangy tomcat, his tail half stripped of hair, was limping his way down the middle of the street. Otherwise, there wasn't a person in sight.

"Hi. What are you doing here?"

"Do you have a few minutes?"

"Uh... Not really, I have a lab at eight o'clock."

"Oh! Big dissection today?"

"No, that's only in bio. This is a chem lab."

"So, what're you doing in chemistry?"

"We're analyzing samples."

"Samples of what?"

"Depends on the group."

"What about your group?"

"Hamburger meat."

"Whoa! I wouldn't want to see that."

"Some group of clowns is doing sperm."

"You'll have to let me know how that one goes."

He winked as he pulled the beautifully contoured rump of his Mazda MX-3 to the curb. Then he got out, walked over to my car and stuck his head through the passenger-side window, only inches from my face. Our eyes were level.

"I've got an offer for you."

The violet collar of his perfectly ironed shirt stood out against the black of his blazer. He smelled like lavender—to match colour with scent, I imagined. His sideburns hugged the curve of his jaw, culminating in a perfectly aligned set of teeth that shined like polished jewels. A work of art. I had to suppress yet another urge to reach out and touch him.

"An offer?"

"One you can't refuse."

For obvious reasons, he couldn't be asking me to marry him. Pity.

"I've almost finished up at the Vanier restaurant. I'm leaving on Saturday. They're sending me over to Sainte-Foy to the Manhattan next. And I need you."

"Me?"

"I have a shitty manager to replace."

"Manager?"

"Five hundred a week."

"I don't understand."

"You'd be perfect."

"Full-time?"

"Yes."

"But I'm in school. I've got three exams just this week, and I'm already having a hard time..."

"Do your exams and then come with me."

"YOU OKAY, LAURIE?" came a yell from above.

Up on the balcony in a yellowed wifebeater, my father was leaning over to make sure I wasn't taking candy from a stranger.

"IT'S FINE, DAD. HE'S MY BOSS!"

"YOUR BOSS?"

"HELLO, MR. GAGNON!"

"HE'S THE GUY FROM TORONTO, THE ONE I TOLD YOU ABOUT! GO BACK INSIDE, I'LL EXPLAIN LATER!"

Bosses don't make house calls for just anybody. Or for just any reason. My father hesitated, then went back inside. Half the neighbourhood had their noses glued to their windows, eager for any excuse to spice up their day — a lingering kiss, a lover's quarrel, a kidnapping.

"I can't..."

"Five fifty."

"But I don't want to work in a restaurant full-time!"

"Six hundred."

"I can't..."

"Six fifty, final offer. You'd be able to fix your car."

He smiled with his eyes. Being all-seeing was just one part of his job, and he knew I had no idea what I wanted to do with my life. We'd talked about it a few times over a glass of white. I thought about my parents and their dead-end jobs: the runs to the scrapyard, my mother's chamber pot, my father's mangled hands. Estelle's faded beauty against the fake Italian decor of the restaurant.

"There's a chance I could be a waitress soon."

"Is that what you want to be? A waitress?"

"So I can go to school, yeah. The money's better. I'm thinking of getting an apartment with my friend Sonia next year."

"Okay then. Come with me, and I'll make you a waitress at the Manhattan."

Upper Town. I'd have to take the 40, then the A-740 to Boulevard Hochelaga, which cut right through the university on its final stretch up the hill, bisecting its departments: plants on one side, humans on the other. I agreed to do a trial run the following day at noon. There was nothing binding about a trial run, so we promised not to say anything at the Italian place. I could afford to skip a history class; I knew that the professor, inclined

towards introspection, would simply read aloud passion-
ately from the book he'd published and made the entire
class buy.

Everything about the restaurant matched the chic
images I'd conjured from books and TV: in the muted
atmosphere of crystal light fixtures, men in suits sat in
leather booths, chatting as they swirled expensive wine
in delicate stemware. A plush carpet muffled the sound
of the waitstaff's shiny shoes as they made their way
back and forth across the spacious room, hands laden
with plates of filet mignon and duck breast. I recited
one of the menu items under my breath, just to taste
it: *Manhattan Potato: jacket potato with a sour cream and
lardon filling, garnished with fresh spring onions.* The servers were handsome and smiling, the uniforms classy, the
setting charming. Even the manager's name, Philippe,
had a princely feel. A woman seated at the bar was
eating a warm goat-cheese salad with pine nuts and
sipping white wine as she flipped through the pages
of a thick file. She could have been Roman's mother.
At the thought of my father's mustard toast, I darted
towards the back.

In the flesh, Philippe was nothing like the affable,
kind man I had envisioned. His office shared a wall with
the kitchen, which was as noisy and messy as every

restaurant kitchen, regardless how fancy the place, just before the lunch rush descends. I could tell he was annoyed the moment I darkened his door.

"Oh, right... the new girl... even though we're not hiring..."

"..."

"You've waited tables before, I assume?"

"Uh... no, not officially. But when I worked on the floor, I used to clear and run food a bunch, to help out the girls..."

He held his head with both hands. My digestive tract seized up and my mouth went dry.

"You can shadow Sandra for lunch. The tall one with dark hair."

My lips stuck to my teeth and I had to stretch the words exaggeratedly just to get them out.

"Uh... Okay. But I don't have a tie or an apron."

"Ah, crap! Look, I don't have time for this right now. I'll grab you one from the back in a minute."

"Where can I find Sandra?"

"I don't know. Try *looking*."

I felt like telling him that assholes wouldn't last long in these parts.

After I'd meticulously checked the kitchen and dining room, I finally came across a girl with a huge chest and blue-black hair stocking the fridges behind the bar. Like all the other servers, she was gorgeous. Judging from the eye roll she threw me in place of a greeting, I figured my initiation had begun.

"I'll tell you right now, I don't split tips with trainees."

"Fine with me."

"Got an order pad?"

"Yes, but I don't have an apron."

"Go ask Philippe."

"He said he'd grab one later."

"Okay. Go! Table twelve just got seated, right over there."

She nodded to indicate the direction.

"We have section E—table ten, right here, eleven, twelve, and thirteen. We also have the three two-tops in section G up on the mezzanine. The trays are here, the water glasses and pitchers are in the service station over there. I'll let you take their drink order. Think you can handle that?"

I placed two glasses of water on a tray. Scarcely ten minutes ago I'd been sitting in my car, scared shitless, and now I was charging across the dining room, hands shaking, towards two men in black suits and mobster haircuts.

"Hello!"

They were completely engrossed in their conversation. I waited a few seconds, then tried again.

"Hello!"

"...but it's totally different with a clause like that.

You'll never be able to argue the client couldn't represent himself."

"Uh...Hello!"

"That's what I've been telling you all along. Don't get them started, or they'll never let it go—"

"HELLO!"

They stopped mid-conversation, their eyebrows gathered in surprise above their noses. I took a mini-step back.

"What is it?"

"Umm...excuse me. Can I get you started with something to drink?"

"The usual, just ask Nancy."

"Uh...Okay. Thanks."

I went back to the computer to wait for Sandra, who was busy taking orders from the two-tops and smiling with the assurance of someone in complete control. The room had suddenly been invaded by diners looking for a quick meal, and the staff was hustling to fulfill their every desire. Sandra came back, practically running.

"What are you doing? You have to follow me! I can't show you anything if you just stand here. Did you take drink orders on twelve?"

"They said 'the usual' and to ask Nancy."

"God, they're so full of it. They act like they're such hotshots...Nancy isn't here, and I don't know what they want. Go back, you might as well take their full order while you're at it. Your training code is eight-seven-two-four. You know how Gamma works?"

"Yeah, we had the same system..."

"Great! Wait for me before you punch in the order, you have to add the cooking instructions and sauces separately."

I returned to table twelve with my stomach in knots.

"Uh...excuse me."

"It's not a big deal, we'll slip him the old ones. He won't even notice."

"Pardon me!"

"Our beers?"

"Nancy isn't here."

"And?"

"I'm here to take your drink order. And your food order, too."

In my naive little head, I'd imagined the training would include a thorough explanation of the menu, like at the Italian place. I crossed my fingers, hoping the names of the dishes would be in French or, at the very least, in English.

"Eight ounce rare, fries, veggies, glass on tap, litre of red."

"Same, hold the veggies. Split the wine on the bill."

Now beat it, kid. I could hear it in the way his fingers swept the air, as if he wanted to sweep me away, too.

I rushed off to find Sandra before I forgot what I still remembered of his order: rare, tap, red...

"How much red do they want?"

"A litre. Fries, beer on tap, veggies."

"What size beer?"

"A glass each."

"Identical meals—real classy! Order the beers and the litre of red from the bar, I'll let you bring them over. Then go greet the couple up on twenty-four before they move to a booth, it's the two up on the mezzanine. When you get back, we're dropping table thirteen. Joey's swamped, so we're taking his seventeen."

In the hours that followed, I bore my cross like that, never knowing where to stand, what to do, or how to hold things. My body just couldn't get the feel of it. It was like I had too many arms and legs, and not enough co-ordination. The cork of the only bottle I tried to open broke apart, stuck halfway down the neck. Sandra practically snatched it out of my hands. I was a klutz who made everyone nervous, including the customers. Philippe sailed by, flitting from table to table with his smile pasted on, ostensibly ignoring me. All I wanted was to hop in my Pony and drive away, to tear down the hill and race back to my own shithole.

In the minuscule staff room where we cashed out after the lunch shift, the ashtray was overflowing with half-smoked cigarettes. Servers would take turns sneaking off during the rush to take a drag from a single lit cigarette—whoever finished it had to light another one in order to keep the eternal flame of the smoke break burning. Since I had nothing to do but wait for my next instructions, I tried to count them without touching the ashtray. At the very least, it made me feel busy. One of the servers came over to take a puff and asked me who I was.

"Cool lipstick, Laurie!"

"Thanks. It's, uh . . . burgundy."

"You gonna be the bossgirl?"

"Nah, a server."

"What the hell? We're already over-staffed. I need more shifts!"

"Don't tell Philippe, he'll send you packing," Laurie said.

Twenty-two cigarettes of three different brands were smoked in the staff room that day. I worked two-and-a-half hours and earned zero dollars. I refused the five-dollar bill Sandra handed me; she'd warned me at the start of my shift that trainees didn't get paid. She didn't insist.

I'd been foisted on an overstaffed restaurant that didn't need another server, and where the last thing anyone wanted was to be spied on by the new boss's little protege, which explained my cool welcome. If Claude cleaned things up here, the way he had at the

Italian place, there's no doubt I'd be accused of being a mole. Persona non grata. I'd never been able to describe my situation in so few words. Suddenly, I longed for the fake grapevine and the customers who dressed up, tacky though their choices were, to come eat spaghetti Bolognese.

I slipped into my car like it was a hot bath. I locked the doors, reclined the seat, and sank back until I calmed down. Then, hidden in a corner of the underground parking lot, I cried like a baby.

I didn't have the courage to report back to Claude in person as planned. His charm didn't travel as easily through the telephone.

"It won't work. I can't do it."

"Why not?"

"Everyone hates me."

"But I'm coming to clean things up."

"Yeah, and then they'll all think I'm a snitch!"

"Oh, come on..."

"Plus, there aren't enough server shifts as it is! Everyone wants more!"

"But there will be."

"The customers are obnoxious!"

"There are assholes everywhere. Dinner's totally different from lunch, you'll see."

"It's not just that..."

"Oh?"

"It's not for me."

"What isn't? Being a server?"

"No, no. The place is just too...chic."

"Compared to what?"

"I dunno..."

"You?"

"Maybe, yeah."

"But you're chic, Laurie. Elegant, inside and out."

"Well, I don't feel that way."

"I should give you the number of my shrink."

"Pff...I'll stay at the old place."

"What did you think of Philippe?"

"He's a dickwad."

My mother wasn't in her booth as usual. I could have really used a few minutes inside with all the smells, the violets, the caramels. Stéphane, the night guard who was filling in for her, had nothing reassuring to say.

"Is she sick?"

"Nope, top shape."

"Where is she, then?"

"She had an appointment."

"What kind?"

"Couldn't tell you. Not my place to ask."

His glass eye was staring at something above my shoulder. I tried to focus on the other one.

"What time did she leave?"

"Dunno, she's been gone a while now..."

"Did she call out, or was it planned?"

"Planned. Got all dolled up and everything. She'll be back later."

"Back from where?"

"How should I know? She's your mother, why don'tcha ask her?"

I ignored the cars honking impatiently behind the barrier while Stéphane let me take a handful of candy in the shape of tools—they didn't hold up well in the heat and would be gone from the shelves once summer hit. Then I rushed over to the garage to try to catch my father.

The guys were working with the doors open, though it was only a few degrees above zero. They couldn't stand being cooped up without proper ventilation and light. They looked a little like miners emerging from the depths, drawn towards the sun, drinking in its brightness.

The calendar of the world's most beautiful cities I'd given to them as a peace offering after ripping up their bimbos was hanging above the Mastercraft. This month, Barcelona proudly flaunted its curves.

"Is my dad around?"

"I'm up two bucks if he gets here in the next three minutes."

"Okay, I'll wait."

"Someone left a message for you."

"For *me*? Who?"

"A customer."

"What kind of message?"

"In an envelope."

"Where is it?"

"Go ask Ron."

Ron was in the cockpit smoking a cigarette and leafing through his Honda bible, squinting against the smoke that rose up and licked his face.

"Hey now! If it isn't Blondie!"

"You have a message for me?"

"I do! Hang on a sec, it's here somewhere... from the guy who came in to get his radio fixed."

He handed me an envelope that was losing its whiteness to the grime of oily fingerprints. The sticky flap had been torn halfway.

"You opened it?"

"Bob did. Just a little."

"But it's for me!"

"There coulda been something dangerous inside."

"Like what? TNT? It's a stupid piece of paper! You're a bunch of gossips..."

"We didn't wanna take any chances, there's some sick people out there."

"Well, what does it say?"

"I can't remember."

"Okay, so everyone read it, not just Bob?"

He buried his nose in the auto-parts manual and pretended not to hear me. I drew a hand giving the finger in the grime-caked glass door. Then I walked over to the calendar and flipped it up. Underneath, the nudes were still there, garage babes with pouts and exaggerated curves. April was clutching a windshield as she stuck out her ass, seemingly ready for action.

"That's what I thought..."

"We're keeping 'em warm."

"You lost your two bucks, Bob. And the next time you stick your nose in my business, I'll kick your ass! All of you!"

From across the room, I could hear them saying something about how the dye had messed with my brain.

"At least I *have* a brain!"

I couldn't wait any longer for my father. The letter was burning my fingertips.

I didn't open it until I had parked near the college.

Hi,

I forgot to say: the blond looks good on you.

I owe you a poutine. Whenever you want.

Between the message and his signature, he'd drawn a little four-panel comic strip. 1. Stick-figure girl with long hair standing on a cube with a circle in the middle — a speaker? — with her arms raised. 2. The girl holding hands with a stick-figure boy on what must have been a sidewalk, judging by the lines that looked like expansion joints. 3. Big stick-figure boy vomiting in thick pen strokes onto the pair of them. 4. A stick-figure boy walking pathetically — head detached from the body for emphasis — next to a rectangle placed over two circles with a smaller rectangle on top. A taxi. Just below, a telephone number. Presumably of the headless stick-figure boy.

In my philosophy class, microcosm of a windowless classroom packed with smelly young adults, Mr. Savary's eager voice made it seem like the world was filled with great thinkers who could save us from human folly by means of a few well-turned sentences. Since Montesquieu claimed there was no distress an hour's reading would not relieve, I tried to forget I'd just royally bungled my new job by rereading Roman's note a thousand times.

9

"My mom has a boyfriend. Can you believe it?"

"What's he like?"

"Dumb as a brick and ugly as sin."

"What does she see in him?"

"He takes her to dinner on weekends. She claims he looks like Clint Eastwood."

"Yeesh."

"If Clint Eastwood was punched in the face... And kept telling boring, pointless stories."

"Does she still want to move?"

"She's starting to talk about moving in with him."

"Where's that?"

"Where does a critter like that live?"

"I dunno, Beauport?"

"Try the asshole of the world: Val-Bélair."

"Shit..."

"Exactly. No way I'm moving there."

"We'll find something, Sonia."

"Should we look in the Upper Town?"

"Too expensive. And I'll be far from work."

"Clint Eastwood says he can get me an interview at a restaurant."

"Which one?"

"It's called Brew."

"Isn't that a bar?"

"They serve food, too. Hamburgers, club sandwiches, stuff like that. They even serve breakfast."

"Oh, cool."

We'd devised a simple plan that was taking a while to come together: 1. I'd become a server. 2. Sonia would take over as hostess. 3. She'd become a server. 4. We would live off our tips in a beautiful apartment with wainscotting and crown moldings. While going to school, of course. Sonia's dream was to become an accountant and make "boatloads of cash," as her mother hoped; I was trying to avoid jobs with the word "mechanic" in the title.

"So, did you call him?"

"Who?"

Eye roll.

"Not yet."

"Come on, scaredy cat! He wrote you a letter!"

• • •

On Claude's last night at the Italian place, the dining room was packed to the rafters. The cacophony was almost enough to drown out the shouts of flustered servers and cooks, whose patience and organization were being put to the test by this sudden rush. It was a perfect night for anybody hoping to pull a dine-and-dash; in the commotion, they should have been able to slip out unnoticed. Should have.

Around 7 p.m., Theresa burst into the kitchen spitting with rage.

"The guy at twenty-seven is gone! The one in the suit with the red face! DID ANYONE SEE THE GUY AT TWENTY-SEVEN? THE ONE WITH THE RED FACE? HE TOOK OFF WITHOUT PAYING, *THE LITTLE FUCKER!*"

The man had shown up alone, dressed in a strange three-piece suit, and had asked to change tables three times. It made sense now; he'd been strategically positioning himself.

As soon as Claude heard Theresa's words, he dashed out to the parking lot. Seeing him leave, the customers swarmed the front window like a school of fish, and everyone watched as he caught up to the thief, who was weaving between cars. Jean-Sébastien, hygienically sporting his hairnet, joined the chase. Estelle was murmuring *Oh my God! Oh my God!* with one hand on her heart and the other on the phone, ready to call the police, while through the reedy speakers Dalida's voice could be heard singing dramatically about Gigi getting her heart broken in America. I walked out with the cooks and a handful of customers who had suddenly lost interest in their meals.

Claude had managed to catch the man and was pinning him to the ground in an armlock. The right sleeve of his jacket had been torn in the preceding scuffle, and the delicate two-tone filigree of his periwinkle shirt was visible. One of the buttons on the jacket sleeve hung limply from a thread.

"Quit squirming or I'll beat the hell out of you!"

"I'm going to press charges! You can't do this!"

"Shut up! You're nothing but a two-bit thief!"

"I just forgot to pay!"

"Do you know who ends up paying for assholes like you?"

"LEMME GO!"

"The waitress does, you bastard! She's the one who pays your bill. HOW MUCH WAS IT, THERESA?"

"FORTY-NINE BUCKS!"

"FORTY-NINE BUCKS, YOU LITTLE SHIT!"

"I JUST FORGOT!"

"I SAID SHUT IT!"

Nobody dared to say a word. The guys from the kitchen had formed a wall around Claude.

"Get out your wallet, and don't try anything. See Jean-Seb over there, with the big muscles? He'll rip your head off. He eats pricks like you for lunch."

"I'll press charges! You have no right..."

"GET OUT YOUR FUCKIN' WALLET!"

The moment the wallet was out, Claude snatched it from him and began emptying its contents on the ground. To everyone's great surprise, it contained nearly thirty dollars in bills and assorted coins, business cards of all kinds, an old key, and a torn photograph. But there was no credit card, which made it impossible to pay the bill in full. Claude took the money and forced the man up. He threw the wallet at him.

"We'll take this cash and you'll owe us the rest. You can drop it off next time you're in the area. There's enough of us here that someone will remember your face. Now get the hell out before the police show up."

The man scampered off without a backward glance. He had the efficient stride of someone used to beating a hasty retreat.

Claude readjusted his jacket — or the pieces of it, at any rate — and wiped the blood that was pooling in one of his nostrils before motioning us back inside. It was hard to say whether he'd been injured during the altercation, or if the blood vessels in his nose had burst under the force of his anger. The police arrived late to the scene and were told they weren't needed: a misunderstanding over an unpaid bill, amicably settled. Everyone took a share of the blame and accepted the consequences, like at the end of a children's book. In the telling, it was almost as if things had ended with a handshake and a pat on the back. The officers managed to overlook both the torn jacket and the crimson droplets speckling Claude's upper lip and left with a wave, glad to have been spared the paperwork that usually ensued with this sort of call.

The crowd disbanded and the restaurant staff got back to work. Everyone would have their own version of the incident, adding in juicy details of dubitable truth until the story became a real whopper. In the most over-the-top version, Claude took out the thief with a Van Damme–style kick.

When he grew tired of answering a thousand and one questions, Claude ducked back into the office to quiet his anger with the help of a few drinks. By the time I walked in, he was so deep in the drunken mists that he'd lost all sight of fake Italy.

"That was one hell of a last shift."

"I wanted to go out with a bang."

"Not hurt, are you?"

He shook his head no and poured me a glass so we could toast.

"How was the hamburger?"

"*So. Gross.* I'm never eating one again. It was practically alive."

"And the other group, the clowns?"

"Turns out sperm isn't edible."

"No?"

"Too high in protein. Passes right through."

"Hah!"

We shot the breeze like that for a while, pushing back the moment of goodbye we were both loathe to reach. I was going to miss Claude a lot, even if I couldn't find the words to tell him. There was almost no chance that the next manager would be this cool.

"Are you sure you don't want to come with me?"

"Nah... It's not really my style, over there..."

"They're just full of themselves, don't let that intimidate you. You're a hard worker. You'll make a place for yourself soon enough."

"But I already have one, here."

He brushed a hand over his face, as if he were chasing away a fly. Loosened up by the wine, he looked suddenly tired.

"You'll miss my incredible fashion sense."

"I sure will."

"And I'll miss your stories about the garage."

"Oh hey, did I tell you about the letter?"

"No..."

• • •

Before leaving, Claude asked me to enter the half-litre of wine the customer had "forgotten" to pay for in the Promos book, which cut the bill to $30. That left Theresa only a tiny tip, but it was the best he could do.

"You know where to find me."

"Uh-huh."

"Come here."

He held me close for a very long time. I inhaled deeply, letting my hands trace the contours of his Terminator shoulder blades through the soft fabric. I loved him, my maximizer, in spite of myself. In spite of everything. Impossible stories have their charm; they line our memories with velvet, a cushion for whenever life proves too harsh.

10

"LAURIE! THERE'S SOMEONE HERE TO SEE YOU UP FRONT!"

"ME?"

"YEAH, A BOY."

"WHO IS IT?"

"JUST GET OVER HERE!"

It crossed my mind, but I didn't believe it until I saw him in the dining room. Estelle found something urgent to do in the kitchen, like an old-fashioned mother trying to marry off her daughter. I stood there with my hands on my stomach, keeping my distance so my end-of-shift smell wouldn't ruin everything.

"Roman?"

He was wearing a navy sweatshirt over a pale-blue tee that was the same colour as the sky, which had finally appeared through the low-hanging clouds after days of grey.

"I thought maybe we could grab a poutine. Or something else."

"How did you find out I worked here?"

"Uh . . . I can't tell you that."

"Can you at least give me a hint?"

"Hmm . . . Okay: 'car.'"

"Pff . . . blabbermouths!"

"I had to torture it out of them. It wasn't easy."

"Uh-huh . . ."

"You're the first girl I've met who has a half-dozen fathers. If you say you've never had a boyfriend before, I'll understand why."

"Who spilled?"

He made an exaggerated coughing sound.

"Ron? Doesn't seem like him."

"He didn't say anything, I guessed."

Estelle stuck her head through the gap in the swinging doors. She let out a little *"Eee!"* before ducking back out again.

"Well, it's a good thing you came. I'm sick of pasta."

"Poutine?"

"But my shift's not over yet."

"I'll wait for you."

"Plus, I don't have anything to wear. I came in my uniform."

"Then we'll get takeout."

"And eat where?"

"Anywhere."

"Okay."

It took me two minutes to close up the office and another fifteen to try to freshen up with wet paper towels and a comb someone had left on the sink. (It was missing a few teeth, but I did inspect the remaining ones to make sure they were nit-free.) I applied/removed/reapplied/re-removed/re-reapplied lipstick, darkened my lashes with mascara, and smiled—a little, a lot, too much, way too much—at the weary looking face in the cracked mirror. It was the best I could do. I begged my inner beauty to amplify the banality of my facial features. In my mother's books, this magic worked on even the plainest women. I deserved it as much as they did.

At least I could get in my car through the right door. For my birthday, which my mother celebrated like I was the queen of England, my father had arranged for the guys at the garage to kidnap my Pony and give it a little makeover. They'd fixed the door, changed the front brakes, and replaced the wipers. Pichette had even given it a wash and stuck a bow in the middle of the windshield, which looked more like golden bird shit than the ribbon in commercials where a woman (never a man) is gifted a new car. I was so touched I almost cried. My mother had wrapped an English-style tea service in flowery paper and placed it on the passenger seat. It was magnificent. If I kept my eyes trained on the lacy designs painted on the edges of the plates, I would never be far from Jane Austen's countryside. No matter which neighbourhood Sonia and I ended up in.

Roman lived in an honest-to-God house. Not an apartment sandwiched inside a cramped building, but a free-standing structure with windows on all sides.

"Let's go in the back, so we don't wake my parents."

We followed the stone path that ran along the west side of the house to a massive side door framed by leafy shrubs. An imposing wooden fence hidden beneath a creeping ivy plant led to the backyard. Even without seeing it, I could imagine the yard boasted a patio for tea parties, benches with sculpted legs, perennials with impossible to pronounce Latin names whose blooms co-ordinated with the seasons, maybe even some rare roses that an expert gardener would tend to using sturdy gloves for protection. All of a sudden, the poutines we were carrying seemed terribly unrefined.

"Is this the staff entrance?"

"It's for the maids and the maintenance workers—the gardener and the driver. The butler and the nanny use the service door on the other side."

"You still have a nanny?"

"I can't help it, I love her too much."

"That's so cute! What's her name?"

"Mary Poppins."

His room took up most of the basement living space. Only the utility cellar robbed him of a few dozen square feet he wouldn't have known what to do with, anyway, unless it was to store even more guitars than he already had. An ingenious arrangement of furniture created a little lounge area at the back, where a floor lamp cast a warm, rich light. The windows were adorned with blue-grey curtains, the walls with bookshelves and healthy looking plants.

"*Wow*. It's big."

"Yeah, but there's two of us."

"Um . . . there's only one bed."

"We share it. Oh, there he is!"

"A cat?"

"Laurie, Jean-Paul. Jean-Paul, Laurie."

"Poor little guy, he only has three legs!"

"Yeah, he's three-quarters of a mongrel."

Roman was studying to be a veterinarian, just like his parents. I was glad I hadn't found this out before, or I might have been interested in him for the wrong reasons. To keep up appearances, I said my father worked in a garage as a parts manager and my mother worked at the hospital in technical support. We all need hubcaps sometimes, to hide the rust on our rims.

"Does it hurt him?"

"Nah, it's an old battle wound."

"Battle?"

"Yeah, against a combine harvester."

"Oh, poor thing!"

"He doesn't remember it."

"Is he old?"

"About a hundred."

"Can I hold him?"

"Sit on the couch, he'll take good care of you."

The animal roused itself and sized me up from the top down before jumping on my lap, landing on its three legs. I took note.

"Dogs usually start from the bottom, but I like the way cats do it better."

"You aren't allergic, I hope?"

"No. Did you save him?"

"With the help of a licenced vet, while I was doing my practicum. We're still not quite sure how he survived."

"He's a miracle!"

"A real hard-head."

"It makes for a good story."

"Uh-huh."

"Why Jean-Paul?"

"My mom's idea. From her soap, *Des dames de coeur*."

"Poor cat, stuck with a namesake like that!"

"He's a slutty cat."

"Hah!"

"Can I get you something to drink with the poutine? A beer? A complicated cocktail? Wine? We have white, red, or blue. Pineapple juice?"

"Blue wine? I'm in."

While I was staring in wonder at his spectacular collection of books, bizarrely arranged by colour, he returned in record time with a glass of blue for me. His was a murky green, like stagnant water.

"What kind of wine is this?"

"*Zinfansmurf.*"

"Ah. And yours?"

"*Frogonnay.* It's cheating a bit, though. We're supposed to follow the order of the colour wheel."

I almost spit my wine out all over him. His delivery was total deadpan, and the more I laughed, the more he kept going. I had to take mini-bites of poutine so I wouldn't spew brown French-fry mush every time I cracked up. His goal was to drink the rainbow, so he served me a glass of indigo next. So long, food colouring. The cat settled itself on my leg, closing its eyes serenely like an otter sunning itself on a rock.

"Your thigh looks comfortable."

"I get that a lot."

"With me, it's the back."

"You have a comfortable back?"

"The back of my hand. My left hand."

"You're a lefty?"

"No."

"You play guitar?"

"Not even."

"Then whose guitars are these?"

"Mine. They're just to make girls think I play the guitar."

"That can't possibly work for long."

"Surprisingly, I always manage to change the subject. Plus, guitars are so nice to look at."

He walked over to a bookcase in the back of the room and began rummaging through a stack of old records.

"You still have records?"

"See? You already forgot about the guitars."

"We'll come back to that."

"I don't like tapes; they don't have a needle that collects dust or makes little *scritches* that add to the song's character. It's not the same."

The record he had gently placed on the turntable started spinning. He lifted the tone-arm, where the needle patiently waited. The *dum...chk*s of "Stand by Me" wafted out of the speakers.

"Madame..."

Roman was standing in front of me, smiling and bopping his right knee in time with the guiro. His head followed along.

"No, no, no..."

"Yes! Come here."

"I don't know how to dance to this."

"You don't need to."

He grabbed my hand and slowly pulled me to him until I was just inches from his nose. Holding me in a position from another era, he nudged my body to follow the suave rhythm of the *dum...chk! Dum, dum, dum, dum...*

"I'll show you the basics: step to the right...step to the left...rock step back. Step, step, rock step..."

"I'll never get it."

"Just follow my lead and let your body rock from side to side...hold your arm a little straighter...yeah, like that...just empty your mind and follow me...close your eyes, you'll feel the rhythm better..."

While Ben E. King begged me to stand by him, I let myself be led and offered no resistance. All I knew about these ancient dances was that they required a degree of surrender that ran totally counter to my nature. In his magic arms, I could almost do it.

When the last *stand by me*s faded out with the music, the record's crackling nibbled away at the silence in the dark room. The ambient noise of traffic outside had stopped, or maybe started up elsewhere. It felt like we were in the airlock of a space shuttle.

"Again."

"The same song?"

"Do you mind?"

"No, no, no!"

We played it about a dozen times in a row. It was too short, anyway, so we were just making it last a little longer. I kept my eyes closed and grooved to the music in his arms. Our feet crossed, drifted apart, and brushed against each other as if they'd had a lifetime of practice. It must have even been pretty to watch. I felt good, so good I could have stood there rocking like that for days on end. Nothing mattered beyond the circle of carpet we were shuffling across.

"Honey?"

A woman's voice drifted down to us.

"Mom?"

I immediately pictured the traditional heroine of my mother's romance novels: slim waist, painted nails, beautifully coiffed hair, smooth complexion — save for a mole on one cheek — silk dressing gown, and matching slippers topped with furry pompoms. The kind of woman who eats warm goat-cheese salads at a mahogany bar. I feverishly hoped she wouldn't come down.

"Can you put on a different song, honey? I'm having trouble falling back asleep."

"Did I wake you?"

"It's fine, sweetie, but just put something softer on so I can get back to sleep."

"Okay, sorry!"

"And hello to the person you're with!"

"Uh... hello, ma'am!"

He half covered his eyes with one hand.

"My mom says 'person' in case I'm gay."

"Are you?"

"No, but one time I told her I was keeping an open mind."

"Shit, we woke your mom up!"

"It's fine, don't worry. Sound just travels far in this house. We'll just put something else on."

"I feel awful."

"She'll fall back asleep, it's okay. I'll put on something with a lot of *doo*s to help her, and I'll turn the volume down low."

He quickly pulled a different record from its sleeve. First a crackling, then some *scritches,* louder this time.

"The *doo*s come in after the first verse, after the whole 'wild side' bit, listen..."

We began dancing again, bodies intertwined, and sang along in whispers until the sun came up. The *doo*s Roman murmured into my ear gave me goosebumps. I thought, *My arrector pili muscles are contracting. I guess some biology lessons really do stick with us.*

The sun found us there, wrapped in each other's arms. I had no idea how to untangle myself. Suddenly the walls were ablaze, and the now-tepid magic wine that had long been forgotten on the coffee table sparkled in the glass. I was drunk on so many other things. Never before had I wanted a night to last as long as I had wanted this one to. I held Roman's beautiful hands in mine and stroked them.

"I have to leave."

"Why?"

"Because . . . it's officially tomorrow. That's how it is in books. Someone has to go. The guy or the girl, it doesn't matter who."

"Why?"

"I don't want your mother to come down with breakfast."

"You're not hungry?"

"No."

"Are you tired?"

"A little."

A thin line of pure white appeared between full lips that were reddening as the temperature in the room skyrocketed. He leaned one of his freckled cheekbones against my forehead as he took my hands in his.

"You can stay and sleep if you want."

"There's already two of you in the bed."

The three-legged cat had long since curled up in a ball, paws crossed over its head. It could have easily been mistaken for a stuffed animal or a big hairy coaster.

"Laurie?"

"Hmm?"

"I wish you'd stay..."

I stared at his lips for a long time, trying to control my breathing. But right before I was about to go for it, I took a step back. I wanted this night to exist, I needed it to exist. It had been the most romantic moment I'd ever read about or watched. He released my hands without much of a fight, and I caught sight of a dimple. He was unbearably handsome.

When I buried my face in the cat's soft belly, all it did was offer me an even larger surface area to lose myself in. It would have been so easy to stay. I flushed at the thought of his beautiful hands on my body.

"Take my jacket."

"I'll be fine."

"Please?"

Rue Saint-Jean was gloriously deserted. I turned left onto Côte du Palais and set off down the hill towards Limoilou. The sun was gleaming on the roof of the train station. The paper boys, still yawning, were hustling along their routes while the cats searched for a quiet place to lick their wounds.

My mother was awake, of course. She sat, one hand swirling the remnants of the instant coffee she'd made in her favourite mug, the other hand resting on a torn paperback. The kitchen was bathed in an orangey glow.

"You weren't waiting up for me, were you?"

"No, no, pumpkin. I couldn't sleep. The sun's so pretty in the morning..."

"Sorry, I should have called."

"It's okay, you'll remember next time. Where were you, sweetie?"

"Oof...I don't know how to explain."

"Look at me...you got stars in your eyes."

"I'm tired."

"Is that all?"

"No..."

The trek over in my Pony had done nothing to diminish the night's magic. I could feel it in every fibre of my body, in the shivers that ran down my neck all the way to my fingertips.

"I guess you don't want to talk about it."

"Oh no, I do. I really do."

"Oh, honey..."

11

On a Friday afternoon three weeks after Claude left, a sign was posted on the front door to the restaurant announcing that it was closed and all employees were terminated, effective immediately. By the time I arrived, a crowd had already gathered in the parking lot. A carefully crafted paragraph cited laws and technicalities, but what was clear was that the days of fake Italy were over and we'd now be going our separate ways, stripped of our adoptive names and characters. Head office would be happy to reassign us to Montreal, where certain locations remained open. There was no mention of the unpaid hours they owed us.

"Fuck you, you bastards!" Jean-Sébastien shouted at the notice. We couldn't have agreed more.

Eyes unfocused, purse hanging from two hooked fingers, Estelle was staring through the front window at the bar, which sparkled back at her. She stood away from the fray, a storm raging below the surface.

"Estelle?"

"Hmm."

"You okay?"

"Uh-huh."

"He could have told you, at least."

"What would it have changed?"

"You could have found something else, or gone with Claude..."

"He didn't ask me to go with him, dear. People don't like old waitresses, makes 'em lose their appetite."

She kept talking to the window without looking at me. It made my stomach turn to admit it, but I knew she was right. No matter how hard she worked, there was just nowhere she belonged anymore. I couldn't come up with anything comforting to say. I kept thinking about the two classes I'd dropped so I could work more hours during the week. The only thing it had done for me was to delay university another semester.

When Jean-Sébastien realized he'd probably never see a cent of the overtime he'd been saving up, he lost it. He backed up as far as possible to build momentum, then ran up and flung himself against the door shoulder-first, like a battering ram, trying to break it down. Unfortunately for him, the hinges and bolts held fast and the frame bore each blow with an elastic firmness. Minutes later Jean-Sébastien was on his back, his elbows skinned.

He picked himself up and found a new target: the brick arch that aimed to give the cheap building a venerable European feel. In under ten kicks, the first fake bricks—imitations glued to a plywood backing—started crumbling in puffs of powder. Estelle stood there, hypnotized, so I led her away by the arm to avoid either of us getting hurt. The others had joined in, driven by the barbaric savagery that animates an angry crowd. Pieces of fake wall were flying in all directions. Minutes later, the entire arch crashed to the ground like a toppled statue. A pathetic fall, befitting of the Empire itself.

"What're you going to do, Estelle?"

"Throw myself off a bridge."

"Estelle!"

"I'm joking, honey! It was a bad joke, I know. And I wouldn't do it that way, anyway, it probably wouldn't work. I'd use pills, less risky."

The bottom half of her face was smiling. The harsh daylight made it easier to see the constellation of fine wrinkles that her foundation only accentuated. The edges of her eyes and mouth were like cracked, dry lake beds.

"I'll make a few calls. I've been old for a while now, I'm starting to get the hang of it. What about you?"

"Bah . . ."

Everyone cleared out once the police arrived. Two officers stepped slowly out of the car, chins in the air, chests plumped, thumbs stuck in leather belts packed with everything needed to survive a week-long special op. They glanced around and mumbled a few words into their two-way radios, then lifted their steel-toed tactical boots with some effort and made their way over to the sign on the entrance door. One of them pointed to the paper as if to say "two plus two is four"; the other took notes on a clipboard, elbows locked against his stomach for support. Then they walked back to their car and left without a fuss.

From the telephone booth at the pharmacy, Estelle called her husband to come pick her up.

"Well, he's not a happy camper! Poor man, having to come all this way . . ."

"Couldn't you just retire?"

"And stay home with that old grump? I'd rather clean houses, scrub prison toilets, label fish in a factory . . ."

The African violets were looking great; the warm weather had thickened the hair on their leaves. I settled into the fold-up seat.

"My God, I wasn't expecting you! What happened?"

"The restaurant closed."

"Power outage?"

"Nope. Door's locked, everybody out on their asses. Game over, *ciao*, bye, go eat shit."

"Holy smoke! I don't believe it! Are they even allowed to do that?"

"Pfft! They can do whatever they want. They don't care about any of us."

"But your Claudio, he must've known!"

"Not necessarily. He's been gone a while."

"Talk about big news, wow! Wait'll your father hears this..."

"If you'd only seen Estelle, Mom. It was so sad..."

"Poor woman..."

Her expression turned serious, her eyes unfocused as she gazed out through window. I noticed pale green on her eyelids.

"You put on makeup?"

"Huh?"

"Are you wearing eyeshadow?"

"Oh! Yeah. I do that sometimes."

"Sometimes? You never wear makeup."

"Sure I do. Every once in a while."

"No, this is new. And there was the other day, too..."

The appointments, the makeup... A lover? Why not? She consumed love stories all day long; it only made sense that her heart might want to beat a little faster. Or maybe it was just spring that made her feel like getting dolled up, wanting to be noticed.

"Here, take some cinnamon fish."

"I don't feel like it."

"I have some banana bread in my lunchbox, but I didn't bring syrup to put on top."

"Do you need a pee break?"

"Thanks, sweetie, but your father came by earlier. If you have time, Cindy'd love to see you. She misses you. Her front teeth are almost grown in. They're crooked, but they're there."

She reached out to take money from a car, supporting her back with the other hand.

"Did you hurt your back?"

"Nah, I'm just getting older. You get stiffer over time, it's one of the worst parts."

"It isn't good to stay bent over like that all day."

"Don't you worry about your old mom."

"You could go see a chiropractor."

"Hey! I have some new books. And I reserved that *Madison* book, remember the one I told you about?"

"No."

"It's coming out in French real soon. I want to be the first to read it. Got pretty good reviews..."

"I just started *The Tin Flute*, so I have to finish that."

"Oh boy! That's not gonna cheer you up! A teeny-tiny apartment on the wrong side of the tracks, a sick kid, that other nut who joins the army...Why don't you take a Barbara? Just three hours, and it'll give your day a different feel. They always have a happy ending."

"I'll check it out."

"Are you going home for lunch?"

"Yeah."

"Good, then you'll be able to tell your father yourself. I'd rather it that way. There's leftover meat loaf in the little Pyrex."

"Okay."

"And don't worry about your job. You know we're not hurting for money. You don't have to work."

"I know, Mom."

"But still, it's sad. I know you liked working there."

"Uh-huh."

"It was bad enough when Claude left...Heard anything from Roman?"

"We spoke yesterday."

"And?"

"And what?"

"Are you going to see him again?"

"Mom, he's all the way in Saint-Hyacinthe."

"So what? You both have cars."

"He's super busy. And so am I."

"You'll have more time now that you don't have a job!"

"I'll find one soon. That reminds me—I have to give Sonia a call. She just started at a restaurant."

"I can talk to Louise, if you want. Her sister-in-law manages the bingo over at the rec centre. She might be able to squeeze you in somewhere."

"Come on, Mom. *Bingo?*"

I was waiting for Cindy when school let out.

"Hey, kid."

"Hey, fatass."

"Are you still pouting? You're not happy to see me?"

"I'm gonna hafta repeat."

"Repeat?"

"Nadine said so."

"Who's Nadine?"

"A bitch."

"Why'd she say that?"

She pulled out a crumpled, half-torn sheet of paper from the jumble of her school bag. A "3/10" was circled three times above a mishmash of poorly scrawled words.

"Whoa there. No one ever teach you to write?"

"Bitch!"

"Hey! Be polite!"

"You, too!"

"Okay, I'll be polite, too. I don't want to hear the word *bitch*. You don't call anyone that."

"You're sooo annoying..."

"Not that, either! No *bitch* or *you're so annoying*, or I'm sending you home."

"Okaaay."

"Was it a test?"

"Naw."

"It was graded, so it must have been."

"Just a dictation."

"You have to *study* the vocabulary words."

"I KNOW!"

"You won't fail the year just for this, but you really have to study..."

"STO-OP!"

"OKAY!"

"You're so mean."

"Don't you have something else to show me?"

"Nope."

"No T-O-O-T-H..."

"LOOK!"

She smiled, pulling back her lips to show me the ridged tips of crooked teeth. I could see tartar buildup already.

"Wow! They look great! Pretty soon you'll be able to eat apples."

"Yuck!"

"Oh stop, you like apples."

"Only with lemon."

"Then we'll make you lemon apples. Feel like doing something special?"

"When?"

"Now."

"*Now*?"

"It's nice out, it's not too hot. We could take a cruise."

"Whassat?"

"A boat trip."

"Where to?"

"I'll explain."

"Wheeere?"

"Not far, we'll take the car on the boat. We stay in the car while we cross."

"But it'll sink!"

"Nah it won't, don't worry. It's a special boat that carries cars. That's what it's made for. Once we're on the boat, we can get out and explore."

"Can we swim?"

"Definitely not. The water's too cold and the boat goes too fast."

"How fast?"

"Normal fast."

"Stoopid."

"The boat has more than one floor, and we can even go see the captain."

"For real?"

"And guess what? There are vending machines!"

"I WANNA GO I WANNA GO I WANNA GO...Did my mom say I could?"

"Anyone's allowed to take this cruise. It's just a little one, it doesn't really count. We'll be back for dinner."

Of course, the ferry was ugly, the captain was a regular guy who didn't even wear a uniform, and the St. Lawrence River wasn't exactly open sea, but she still enjoyed tearing up and down the steep staircases between floors. She was scared of falling, and I was scared she would be blown from the deck by the gusts of wind, but she loved watching the albatrosses glide like cloud princes through the blue sky without batting a wing.

"Look, Laurie! Seagulls!"

"Those aren't seagulls."

"I knowww."

"What do seagulls eat, kid?"

"Uh…"

"Fries. Like at the Kentucky Fried Chicken by our house. Do you see any fries here?"

"Uh…"

"Nope. Nothing but water. So they're albatrosses."

She marvelled at the big frothy fish tail the boat left in its wake, and gobbled up a salty chicken soup from the machine that took — yay! — both big and small change. We made a quick stopover on the mainland (also known as Lévis) before turning around and getting back into the line of cars returning to Quebec City. When she realized the boat we were waiting for had just left without us, Cindy began to panic. It had forgotten us and wouldn't come back, we'd never see home again, her mother would kill her. To calm her down, I exited the line of cars and we came home via the Pierre Laporte Bridge. It was almost as exciting for her as the boat had been.

"See? There are lots of different ways to get home. You just have to trust me. We wouldn't have gone if I hadn't been sure we'd be able to come back."

"Where's the Pont d'Avignon?"

"In France."

"Where's that?"

"We'll go tomorrow."

"Is it hot in France?"

"Not really. But they eat croissants."

"Yuck."

12

Sonia had told me to come to the restaurant at 4:30 to meet the manager before the dinner rush. Though she'd only been working there a little over a week, she'd gotten me an interview somehow. In my nine months at the Italian place, I'd never managed to do as much for her.

I stood on the sidewalk looking dubiously up at the restaurant sign: a doll-like girl sculpted out of neon lights was holding a pint of beer twice the size of her head. Her cleavage burst from under her chin like a pair of butt cheeks.

Another neon sign that simply read *O'Keefe* welcomed customers inside the gloomy foyer. At least there was no brass railing that needed constant coats of Brasso, so I guess it evened out. The walls were hung with posters advertising other beers, flashing dart boards, and dusty mirrors. There were slot machines in one corner. A young woman appeared carrying a bar glass rack on one hip. She set it down on the counter, then walked over to me.

"Hi! Here to eat?"

I refrained from asking what the other options were.

"No."

She had very long hair and wore it loose, perfectly free to fall into a plate and get stuck in the brown gravy of a hot chicken sandwich (Sonia had encouraged me to memorize the restaurant's top sellers so it would seem like I knew my way around). Her eyelids sagged under the weight of false lashes and a thick layer of lapis lazuli shadow. Her dizzyingly low-cut top revealed an even tan. *Destiny*, according to her name tag. It must have sounded fancy in French.

"I'm here to see Jean-Pierre."

"Wait here, lemme go check."

Her four-inch heels made her legs look even longer, and her hips swayed back and forth in time to each perilous step. It was hard to picture her dashing around in the middle of a rush, arms loaded with metal trays of wobbly plates. Sonia emerged from the kitchen in front of her.

"Hey! You're here!"

She was still tying her apron, which held a notebook

and three pencils. No corkscrew. There was something not quite right about her uniform, but it took me a few moments to pin down what it was.

"Jean-Pierre isn't in yet, but like I said, he seemed super-interested when I told him about you."

"Wow! Check out that cleavage!"

"It's the uniform."

"But you don't serve in that, right?"

"'Course we do, why?"

"Come here. Holy . . ."

"It's not *that* bad."

"You're not wearing a bra."

"No."

"Why not?"

"We just don't wear them."

"What do you mean, 'we don't wear them'?"

"Oh, come on! My boobs are so tiny, a bra wouldn't even make a difference."

"But that's not the point!"

"You sound like my mom."

"JEAN-PIERRE'S NOT HERE YET!" Destiny hollered over at us.

Sonia gave her a thumb's up and Destiny ducked back through the swinging doors.

"You're really not allowed to wear a bra?"

"No. We have to let our tits swing loose, but who cares? The light's so dim here, you can't tell, anyway."

The cover of the menu showed three girl-objects—
a blonde, a brunette, and a redhead—handing me a
pint of beer. I clearly wasn't the target audience, since
nothing had ever made me feel less like reaching out.
Or having a drink, for that matter.

"If you can't tell, then why not wear one?"

"Who cares? Let it go! Those are the rules, end of
story."

"Come on. We're leaving."

"Oh, stop it, Lau..."

"Grab your things, we're getting out of here."

"Lau, it pays."

"It pays? So does pole dancing! So does giving blow
jobs!"

"Hey, whoa! I serve food!"

"To dirty men who picture your hard little nipples
while they jack off in the bathroom between bites of
club sandwich."

"Honestly..."

"I bet they grab your ass when you walk by, eh?"

"Look, do whatever you want. I have to go set up
my section."

"Oh, I get it! They just bump into you by accident..."

"Then go find us another waitressing job!"

"We don't have to be waitresses."

"Wait, now you're the one saying that? *You*? How are
we gonna pay rent?"

"I don't know, but not like this. No way."

"Your veterinarian's turning you into a snob."

"A snob? Because I don't wanna show dirty old men my boobs?"

A man who I took to be Jean-Pierre appeared and started walking towards us. He looked me over as he approached, his eyes shimmering with lust.

"Are you the new girl?"

On the third try, my tongue slipped back into position.

"Are you the pervert manager?"

His mouth was almost entirely covered by his moustache; all I heard was the air as it whistled between the hairs. He stuck out his chest and sucked in his stomach in an attempt to make himself look slimmer. To no avail.

"Lau, you'd better go."

"Is this little punk your friend?"

"Come on, Sonia." I tried to catch her eye.

"Nobody's forced to work here, missy. It's a free country."

"Well, nobody should force girls to work dressed like that."

"This isn't Sunday school."

"Oh, no? Well, too bad, 'cause I think you should go to hell!"

"Now, listen to me. You turn around and walk your ass outta here as fast as you can, before I tell you where to go, cupcake."

"I'm not a cupcake."

"Scram!"

Behind him, Sonia signalled that she would slip out the back. On her way to the kitchen she passed Destiny, who was coming out. I waited until Sonia was gone, then turned and walked away as fast as I could.

"I CAN'T STAY, ANYWAY, I HAVE TO GO CALL LABOUR STANDARDS!"

He didn't follow me, though I gave him the finger behind my back on my way out for good measure. Sonia had walked around the building and was waiting for me by the time I made it through the door. We jumped into the car together.

"You're crazy, Laurie!"

"Thanks."

If this were a movie, we would have taken off, tires squealing and heads thrown back in glee, cackling like witches over the strains of an electric guitar. In real life, some obnoxious car-tire commercial played on the radio while we drove down an unbelievably crowded stretch of road. In my nervousness I'd made a right instead of a left, and Sonia was mad at me for going the wrong way. Despite my fragile satisfaction, as I considered the bridges I'd just burned, I could see I'd have to work hard to clean up the fallout.

"Sorry, but I couldn't help it! That stuff really gets to me."

"..."

"There are lots of other jobs out there, Sonia."

"..."

"What exactly is Clint Eastwood's connection to that shitty place?"

"I dunno."

"Well, he might be banned now."

"Doesn't matter, he can go to hell."

After weeks of fruitless job searching, I finally swallowed my pride and called Claude at the Manhattan. But he had already moved on. Half the team had been fired. A smooth Normandy landing. I hoped, despite myself, that Philippe had been one of the soldiers to fall. Nobody knew how to reach Claude, but they wouldn't have told me, even if they did. "That's private information, miss. We hope you understand."

In the double gymnasium at the rec centre, dozens of tables had been set up at semi-regular intervals on the hardwood floor, relegating the coloured lines to abstract patterns that all were free to cross. Although the caller wouldn't start the bingo for another forty minutes or so, people were already finding their seats and lining up their good luck charms—if that's what you could call the karma necessary to win a portable vacuum cleaner in the shape of a mouse, or a set of god-awful cookie jars. Beside their scorecards, little old ladies (along with two or three invisible men) began to set out Virgin Mary figurines, devotional medals, and all kinds of oddly shaped vessels that likely held baby teeth, hair clippings, or the ashes of a loved one. Though embodied in an array of cheap junk, their piety was sincere.

"Here's how it works: you get here at six, you set up 'til six thirty, you wait tables 'til nine thirty. After everyone leaves, you clean up the tables and the service area, then help everyone restock the kitchen 'til it's filled to the brim and looks so shiny it could be in a magazine. You leave once everything's done, between ten fifteen and ten thirty."

Madame Deslauriers was as wide as she was tall, an equilateral slab of a woman whose contours had long since dissolved into the uniform, compact shape of her body.

"Hélène does the bathrooms, so don't you touch 'em. But watch her do 'em so you can learn—I wouldn't be surprised if she takes off soon, same as Melanie. She's the girl you're here to replace. I'll tell ya' one thing, these girls have no idea how good they got it here ... Oh, and I dock your mistakes from your fifteen dollars a night. You flub up, you pay for it."

"Can we eat our mistakes?"

She looked at me thoughtfully, as if she wanted to see whether I could use the food or not.

"That's a nice colour ya' got there. Did Louise fix it up?"

"Yeah, but the roots are a bitch."

"Get used to it, girlie. You'll have to dye it once you go grey, no choice."

Madame Deslauriers would've gotten along well with Ron, whose philosophy was simple: *Life is hard. You stick it out, you keep sticking it out, and then you die.*

"You get to keep your tips. You've waitressed before, so I'm not too worried about you."

I'd never officially been a waitress. She knew but didn't care.

"The kid's gonna train you, so listen good. She's a fast one."

"The kid" couldn't have weighed more than a hundred pounds. She had blond hair (natural, you could tell), a toothy smile, and the enthusiasm of someone who'd just won the vacuum cleaner. She was like a smaller version of me. Physically, anyway.

"Hi! I'm Joe."

"Laurie. I thought your name was Hélène..."

"It is. Joe's my other name."

"Uh...okay."

"The new girl always takes the last row, the one at the back. It's a pain in the ass having to go so far, I know, but you'll get used to it. I did it for a long time, it's not so bad. Just ignore everyone in the other rows, even if they call your name. You got a lot of people to take care of already, twenty long tables full . . . Well, not as full as they used to be, but still."

"Why not?"

"They're old, they die. Young people don't like bingo as much."

"I can see why. It's boring as hell."

"You gotta use a seating chart or come up with a trick to remember orders. I make three columns: table number, name — I know everyone's name — order. Melanie wasn't good with names, so she'd write stuff in the second column like 'big tits' or 'triple chin.'"

"Hah!"

"That's how the guys in the kitchen call it, too. 'Egg salad for dog-face!' Madame Deslauriers really didn't like that, but Melanie was our best seller, so she didn't say anything."

"You never rotate sections?"

"Nope."

"Don't you ever feel like switching things up to make it fairer?"

"No. We never get any new faces around here, so it's easier to stick with the same people. They tend to order the same thing."

"Where'd Melanie go?"

"To a real restaurant."

"Where?"

"Upper Town."

People who said "Upper Town" usually came from the Lower Town. In Joe's case it showed in her diphthongs and garbled vowels.

"Are you going with her?"

"She's gonna try to get me in, soon's I can."

"How old are you?"

"Almost eighteen."

I held back a laugh. The girl was fifteen, tops. If we were rounding up.

"Here's your tray."

"This? But it's a cafeteria tray."

"That's right. You gotta hold it with both hands. You can either take the stairs or the elevator. I always take the stairs, elevator's too slow."

"Helluva detour."

"Do what you want, it's your call. Come on, I'll show you your section."

Excitement was quietly building in the crowded gymnasium. Once people sat down, they were stuck; the almost unhealthy care they gave to placing their objects made it impossible to move around. This allowed me to draw a Battleship-inspired seating chart on which I would note orders using my own shorthand system. For multi-item orders, such as burger with the works/

fries/Coke, I would sketch an atom with Bw (burger/ works) as the nucleus, adding little feet for the sides (f and C). Once an order was delivered, I would erase it. It might look like a periodic table, but my floorplan would work like a charm.

My foolproof plan had given me a little too much confidence. I wanted to show off by pretending my tray was a real one, holding it with one hand and stabilizing it from underneath with my fingers, spread like an octopus's tentacles. It should have come as no surprise, then, when my humiliation matched my pretentions. The first time I overturned my tray was on the stairs, spilling everything into a pile of semi-solid mush. The second time was between tables seven and eight, when an old lady who was just trying to help reached for her coffee and threw me off balance. Okay then, two hands it would be. But despite this wise resolution, I still wound up on all fours when I slipped in a puddle of melted ice (which I had failed to clean up from spill number two) and fell chest-first into a large poutine. When I looked up at the digital scoreboard, the time was only 7:30. Hélène was looking at me, her eyes full of pity.

"You're getting better with the tray, at least!"

You can't get by in the jungle with nothing but a rectangular piece of plastic; I was feeling a little overwhelmed. I didn't make a cent that night, but

Madame Deslauriers agreed to wipe my slate clean. She couldn't imagine anyone having to pay to come to work.

"You can eat your mistakes once you learn not to dump them on the ground."

"I just had a hard time with the deliveries..."

It made me happy to see her laugh. Hélène had insisted we share a family-sized poutine and wouldn't take no for an answer, so I eventually relented.

"This way, you get more than if you ordered two regular poutines. I won't touch the fries on your side, promise. I used to do this a lot with Melanie. Do you put ketchup on 'em?"

"Yuck!"

"Good, me neither."

We ate in the parking lot sitting in my popped trunk, listening to music. At some point we figured out that Hélène had delivered newspapers to my family's doorstep "when she was little." Our paths had never crossed; I'd never been awake early enough. There was something endearing about her. Kind of like Cindy.

"I wanna have a car, too, some day."

"The car isn't the expensive part. It's the maintenance and all the rest that's the problem."

"I don't have my licence yet."

"I guess you're not sixteen."

"Almost."

If I stuck with bingo for a few weeks, I'd be able to write "server" on my resumé with a clean consciousness. Unlike Hélène, I was scrupulous about not stretching the truth.

Three Wednesdays later, when I finally had Section 4 under control and I knew all my customers' names by heart, Madame Tomassin from Section 2 collapsed. She had an angina attack as the crowd reached fever pitch, their loud *"Aaah!"*s somewhere between disappointment and joy as each number was called. Women whose weathered fingers had known life before washing machines were frantically rubbing rabbits' feet or bits of cloth, while the commotion from Madame T's fall swelled until it reached the caller's podium. The game was temporarily put on hold, much to the chagrin of ladies who were eager to attain earthly bliss in the form of a goose-shit khaki recliner. Evidently, Leon's Furniture Warehouse hadn't found a colour-blind buyer. Donated to the bingo, the chair could be written off as a loss. One could almost see past the colour if the recliner were paired with a nice throw, the most level-headed players told themselves.

The paramedics arrived in under five minutes. I went weak at the knees when I saw the man with the scar breeze in wearing his handsome uniform. Hélène's knees were shaking with joy.

"Cool! It's Fred!"

"Who?"

"The paramedic. The taller one. The cuter one."

"You know him?"

"Yeah, we go way back...he always comes to our rescue."

She had the glow of a great romantic, and I was reminded of Anne of Green Gables. Passionate souls have to exist in real life before they can turn up in books. The word "our" seemed to cast a wide net.

"I *so* wish I could faint all the way."

"What do you mean, 'all the way'?"

"I almost fainted once, but I didn't go all the way. And he didn't pick me up; Roger did..."

"Who's Roger?"

"My neighbour. But he died."

"Ah. I fainted the other day."

"Did you go all the way?"

"Yeah."

"Lucky! Where were you?"

"In a church."

"Oh my God! What a great place to faint! Oh, wow...with the stained glass and the organ and everything...What happened?"

I didn't want to burst her bubble. It didn't seem fair to have had everything—the perfect faint and the revered saviour.

"I fell."

"And then what?"

"I got up."

"Did you bust your head open?"

"No, it was a pretty graceful fall."

"And then what?"

"I went home."

"Bo-ring. Well, at least you didn't pee your pants. I hear that can happen."

In no time at all, the paramedics had the patient wrapped up and loaded into the belly of the ambulance. Death must not have come knocking this time around; the sirens didn't make a peep. Fred bowed to Hélène theatrically. He hadn't recognized me; I figured it was the hair. The interlude, though short, had prevented the stars from aligning and thrown luck off its course. From all around the room came the grumbles of players who had just missed out on the jackpot. Life is unfair. You stick it out, and then you die.

large flowerpots, lit from behind, led to a pergola in the middle of the yard. Small groups of people were gathered under the golden domes of propane patio heaters. I hid in the darkness of the house's western wall, which was covered in Virginia creeper, and watched the scene, unnoticed. The tip of my foot slipped into the light and turned yellow. I pulled it back.

One of Roman's hands held a beer, and the other had disappeared into a pocket, giving him a laid-back vibe. A girl with jet-black hair stood in front of him. She was saying something funny with one hand; the other held a glass of white wine. No doubt something expensive. She was nearly as tall as he was, with a slender waist, radiant skin, and big blue eyes. Drop-dead gorgeous, breathtakingly majestic. Her rings caught the light and refracted it into a thousand tiny rays that glittered in the night. Another girl in a white fluffy top put her hand on Roman's shoulder. Two seconds of suspense. Her curls scarcely moved. She was saying something important with her head lowered, eyes looking up. Then everyone burst out laughing, apparently thrilled by her sense of humour. I took two steps back. I wouldn't have gotten the joke. It was probably in English, or it turned on some expression I'd never heard before. It would have gone over my head and I would have looked stupid. Stupid, ugly, insignificant. The prettiest thing about me was my name, and that alone wasn't enough to show up at a party full of such glamorous, intelligent strangers. I couldn't do it.

"Hi! Did you just get here?"

"Oh, God!"

"Sorry, I didn't mean to scare you."

"No, no, it's me, I..."

A natural blonde with teeth unnaturally white and straight, lips like candy. Even in the half-light, she positively glowed. Eyes so pale they were almost translucent, set in skin so milky I could barely see it. She reminded me of a jellyfish.

"Are you looking for someone?"

"Uh...no."

"I'm Florence."

"Oh..."

"Who're you?"

"Laurie."

"Are you friends with Bernard?"

"No, I don't know him."

"This is his house."

"Oh!"

"Who'd you come with?"

"Uh...I'm supposed to meet Roman."

"Hang on! You're the girl from the garage?"

The ground opened beneath me and I fell into a hole as wide and as deep as the pit. I watched myself tumble through the grimy windows of the garage office. My heart came unstuck, my lungs collapsed, and the rest followed, plummeting silently through the humiliation. A sea of oil pooled in my head, drowning me in reverse, from the top down.

On the surface, however, the envelope held. I managed a smile and improvised an easy out.

"I forgot something in my car—I'll be right back."

"Okay! See you soon!"

The darkness spit me out onto the newly paved asphalt of the deserted street, where only the slight rise of the manhole covers interrupted the perfect smoothness. I ran to my Pony without looking back. With any luck, they'd be waiting patiently for me to return to the party.

Later, as I looked out over the Lite-Brite city from the parking lot of the church on Côte d'Abraham, I played Depeche Mode's *Violator* on loop and pictured myself floating over the rooftops until I calmed down. I arrived home heavy-hearted, my mind clouded with doubt.

"I'm telling you, Mom, nothing happened."

"But, sweetheart, Roman's looking everywhere for you!"

"He called here?"

"Sure did, he said someone at the party saw you, but then you took off..."

"I know, it's complicated."

"We started worrying when you didn't come home,

either. Your father called Jingle, got all the guys on the radio out lookin' for you..."

"Oh no! I went, but I didn't stay. I wasn't feeling good, that's all."

"Not feeling good how?"

"My stomach, I got queasy..."

"You could've told Roman, seeing as you were there."

"I left in a hurry. I was feeling sick."

"What in God's name were you doing this whole time?"

"I lay down in the car and waited for it to pass."

"You could've called your father."

"For what?"

"He'd 'a brought you back. You coulda slept in your own bed, then gone out to get the car tomorrow."

"No, no, I'm fine. I'd rather have the car with me."

"Well, call your boyfriend, at least."

"He's not my boyfriend. He goes to school on the other side of the world!"

"Saint-Hyacinthe's not so far... Your father and me, back in our day..."

"Aaah! I don't want to hear about your day! Back when everything was super-slow and far away."

She bit back her old stories with a sigh, far more disappointed than me.

"Did something happen with you two? Seems to me..."

"No."

"But you were so happy..."

"It was just a bad day, okay? I wasn't feeling well, that's all."

"And now you're feeling better?"

"Yeah, it passed."

"But you didn't want to go back, not even to see Roman?"

"No, I still don't feel great. I'd rather just rest."

She didn't believe me, of course.

"In any case... He left a number where you can reach him. I should tell your father you're home, he must be worried sick. We feared the worst. My God, if you only knew all the awful things that went through my head... But now you're here, that's all that matters."

"I'm really sorry, Mom..."

I leaned over and hugged her, to comfort us both.

"Oh, baby, it's okay. Careful with my back, sweetheart..."

These days, my mother's hands were permanently affixed to the small of her back, as if to keep herself from falling. The bone setter could no longer relieve her pain, which welled up from inside. Every spasm of worry I inflicted on her crushed the bones a little bit more. I'd kill her if I kept this up. While the crisis was slowly being defused throughout the neighbourhood,

I went up to my room to make a phone call. I could tell Sonia everything.

"Why are you whispering?"

"I don't want my mom to hear."

"Why didn't you stay? You're so into him! What's your problem, anyway?"

"You didn't see them!"

"Who?"

"The girls!"

"What girls? What about them?"

"It's hard to explain."

"Well, I think you're acting like a crazy person."

Later, hidden among the wobbly stack of books on the telephone table, I found our copy of *Love Story*. Jenny's saucy banter would do me good. Two and a half hours' worth. Originally a 3, but my mother had crossed it out and revised her rating. I was already smiling by the time I read the first "Preppie." Two hours and twenty-two minutes later, I was bawling my eyes out as Jenny died on the page. When my mother came over to see what was wrong, all I had to do was flash her the cover. She lowered her eyes knowingly, and I knew she understood. The puzzle was falling into place; the book had supplied the final pieces. I felt guilty and hopelessly pathetic; in her eyes, I was wonderful.

. . .

Roman called several times to check up on me and make sure I was feeling better. The lie made me cagey, and I wove myself awkwardly through the stitches of its netting, tangling myself even further in its ridiculous web. It must have been obvious every time I abruptly redirected the conversation. I didn't know how to get us out.

We didn't see each other again before he left for an internship in Charlevoix. Sonia was right: I was acting like a crazy person.

14

The spring weather had, paradoxically, filled the gymnasium. The caller was about to shower the blue-hairs with numbers lucky enough to win the holy grail, a T-fal deep fryer that would bless some lucky family with the ability to whip up fries, corn dogs, and onion rings in the comfort of their own home. To get the crowd salivating, the box was opened and the thick instruction and recipe booklet left out for all to peruse. It assured would-be buyers that children would clamour for more broccoli and parsnips as long as they were deep-fried. A whole new world of possibility awaited in the stainless-steel basket of this contraption that was not-so-coincidentally dubbed the T-fal *Revolution*.

On that day, my back row included a few defectors: since half the prizes had gone to people in my section the previous week, rumour had it that I possessed some sort of lucky karma. Players wanted to be near me in case it was contagious — though a basic understanding of statistics would have persuaded them to stay far away. And although this re-shuffling was temporary, in the eyes of the faithful it was a betrayal capable of upsetting the divine plan of the already inscrutable bingo gods. And so it was that, under the accusing whispers of a small group of backbiters, Lucie, assistant pharmacist at the Uniprix ("clerk" didn't sound distinguished enough for her), settled into seat E-7, curios and golden calves in tow. I liked Lucie. She was the one who'd suggested replacing the flu suppositories my mother fervently believed in with tablets. She immediately ordered a can of my "icy coldest" Diet Coke, to attain the rank of official customer before the game even started. Best to play by the rules if you wanted luck on your side.

Hélène came over to me, all smiles, even though I'd just stolen two of her regulars.

"Sorry, Joe."

"They're shit for tips, no skin off my back. Plus, see the one in the blue jacket with the big glasses?"

"Yeah..."

"She stinks. Like onions!"

"Oh, okay. So, did you hear anything from Melanie?"

"Yeah, she's good. But it won't work for this summer."

"Why not?"

"Everyone wants more shifts in summer."

"Don't the full-timers take vacation?"

"Yeah, but not enough. No big deal though, I can wait. Did you see the new machine?"

"What machine?"

"Ice cream."

"Regular or soft-serve?"

"You ever seen regular ice cream from a machine?"

"No."

"It's gonna be a shitshow, just wait."

As Hélène had predicted, the ice cream machine created a nightmare. We had to run up and down the stairs and serve customers out of order to keep the cones from melting all over the place. And since we were still waiting for the cardboard stands the supplier had promised, we had to make our own out of old box bottoms. Splatters of melted ice cream dotted the aisles, the stairs, and the elevator button-panel like bird poop. Smooth deliveries were few and far between.

Row 2 won the first game: an Avon starter kit. It didn't appear to upset too many people. I was dropping off the onion lady's coffee-three-creams-three-sugars when Madame Liette in F-4 (my section) won the second game, with a cash prize this time. Murmurs started rippling through the room. But since the poor woman's husband had just left her for a saleswoman at Sears who'd sold him a beautiful Maytag washing machine—for Mother's Day, no less—everyone agreed she deserved a little luck, just this once. When my customer in B-9 went up to collect her crisp fifty-dollar bill for winning the third game, the rumblings grew louder and all eyes turned to me. In another era, they would have chucked me onto a pyre and fed the fire with all the unlucky cards. Half of the grumblers would have gladly decamped to my side if it hadn't been for all the trappings and half-completed cards they would have needed to move. Lucie called me over, twirling an index finger in the air. I'd just served her a fries-and-gravy with extra gravy. Basically a French-fry soup.

"Enough gravy for you?"

"Let 'em whine, honey. Don't you listen, they're just jealous. You deserve all the luck you get, it's gotta balance out somehow. You should sit down and take a card."

"I deserve it?"

"'Course you do..."

There was a touch of compassion in her sad smile, a conspiratorial glimmer whose origins I couldn't place. The ice cream I still needed to deliver was sitting in a glass supported by peas.

"I don't understand."

"Sure you do, doll... what with your mother'n all."

"What about my mother?"

"I didn't tell a soul."

She kept her voice low, the words escaping between teeth coated in brown gravy.

"What haven't you told a soul?"

"You know, about your mother."

"WHAT ABOUT MY MOTHER?"

"Shhh...I know your mother's sick..."

I didn't even try to hold on to the tray. I just let it fall. Everything on it took a four-foot nosedive. The peas that managed to avoid the ice cream rolled across the floor like the beads of a necklace. I ran towards the nearest glow of an EXIT sign. Towards my mother. My sick mother.

"Laurie! Whatcha doing? Laurie? What's wrong?"

Hélène's voice pursued me, but I didn't stop.

I floored it home, took the stairs three at a time, and flew into the living room. My mother was napping, wrapped in the throw that was too soft not to double as a blanket. Her book had fallen between the couch and the coffee table, crumpling the pages. My father was watching television. He glanced down at his watch, then up at my ashen face and serving apron.

"Well, then, I was just about to run to the corner store..."

Slowly, my mother pushed herself to a sitting position. She didn't try to do damage control. I couldn't look at her without sobbing for what she had tried to hide from me.

"My baby..."

"You're sick?"

"Very sick, sweetie."

"What is it?"

"My lungs."

"Cancer?"

"Uh-huh."

"But you never smoked!"

"It doesn't work like that."

"The doctors can fix it, there's treatment..."

"Not for me."

"So you're going to die?"

She closed her eyes and lowered her head.

"When?"

"With treatment... I have a few months left. They said it's aggressive."

"When were you going to tell me?"

"I wanted you to keep living like normal, for as long as possible."

"Normal? But, Mom, you're dying!"

"I didn't want it to be the only thing we thought about or talked about. Or for you to change your plans to move out."

"I had a right to know."

"Don't cry like that, my angel..."

"But it's not fair!"

"It's not, I agree with you there. I had you late, and

I'm leaving early. God trimmed the edges on both sides. It sure seems stingy of 'im."

"You still believe, even now?"

"I need to hate someone, that's a fact...Don't cry like that, baby..."

I wanted to listen, to do it for her, but I couldn't. I cried all evening, all night, and throughout every week that followed, consumed by the pain that somehow kept finding new ways to hurt me with every thought, idea, memory, self-reproach, and regret. In the books my mother devoured, the tears always ran dry sooner or later; in real life, they fell unabated.

A few days later, my father asked me to come with him. I didn't ask questions.

"You can bring the kid."

I hadn't set foot in a salvage yard in years. The mountains of scrap metal and gizmos of all kinds that had dazzled me as a child now inspired a feeling somewhere between indifference and disgust. The piles of tires I used to scale like castle walls were now nothing but big heaps of dirty, smelly rubber rings. But for Cindy, I would turn them into magical volcanoes.

The grassy portion of the car cemetery was smaller than last time I was here. The area around the main office where I had once picked wildflowers had been replaced by Tempo shelters full of pieces of junk I doubted would fetch a quarter apiece. Lying in a heap under a hole-ridden tarp that was flapping in the wind was a jumble of miscellaneous items—ball caps, cassette tapes, even baby strollers that had been pulled from the wrecked cars. Battered cardboard boxes held wet clothes, their synthetic fibres composting in a mixture of sweat and swill. Judging by the thin layer of moss already nibbling the edges, if the wildflowers were to come back one day, this would be the place.

The same man, Phil, still reigned over this kingdom of rust. He never changed, he just dried out and shrank down over time, like a baked apple–head doll. He was the only person I knew whose palms were darker than the backs of his hands.

"The kids wanna go for a ride. Is the tractor free, boss?"

The real attraction of the salvage yards was how my father, loyal customer that he was, had won the right to use whatever machines were on hand to sift through piles of junk and look for parts. In every yard in the area, certain condemned vehicles were refitted and used to haul heavy parts from place to place. They were like the grocery carts of the scrap yard.

"Nah, Nico's using it to grab a differential. Take the Micra, the keys are inside. She coughs a little, but she works. Just gotta play with the choke."

Once we made it to the graveyard section at the very back of the yard, my father got out and handed me the wheel so I could let Cindy drive.

"'S'not even a real car."

"Quit whining."

"It doesn't have doors."

"It's faster to get in and out that way!"

"I wanna drive by myself."

"You have to sit on my lap."

"NO! BY MYSELF!"

"Stop shouting. You're too small, your feet won't reach the pedals."

I let her try, just to save myself some saliva. Even with her tongue out, body twisted, and toes pointed as far as they would go, her feet couldn't touch either pedal.

"I can't ritch."

"*Reach*, not ritch. How do you write that *ea* sound, by the way?"

"Move the seat back, Lau."

"The handle's broken, I can't. Listen, I have an idea."

"A bad one, I bet."

"I'll control the pedals, but..."

"But what?"

"...you can shift the gears. All by yourself."

She opened her eyes wide, two little brown islands floating inside white orbs.

"With the knob?"

"The knob and the stick."

As my father had often done for me, I had her visualize the tree of the gear shift before she practiced doing it with her eyes closed; moving into third gear was always tricky. She took a solemn breath and turned the key—a little too long, the engine protested—then gripped the spongy steering wheel, hands at ten and two. Full speed ahead.

"Don't look at the hood! Keep your eyes up, or you'll go crooked."

"But I hafta look where I'm going!"

"If your eyes stay down, you'll keep zigzagging. Look up and you'll go straight."

We headed towards the small wooded area at the back, and I let her drive over bushes and take turns by herself, just to scare her. Her arms were too short to cross, so she slid them over the wheel in bursts, centimetre by centimetre. The sharp bones of her tiny bum dug into my thighs. She squealed with excitement at every acceleration. For one of the few times since we'd known each other, we were in complete agreement: this was so much better than Disney World. A comparison wouldn't even be worth the trip.

Later, while Cindy was loading a stroller with rocks to run over the worms she'd placed in its path, I sat down beside my father in the bed of a Ford Ranger with our feet dangling over the edge. The truck was overgrown with tall grasses and dandelions. The things nature does when humans don't interfere.

"You said you wanted to move out, so move out."

His words were as poorly wrapped as his gifts. The gnarled hooks of his fingers gripped the metal. Each syllable tortured him.

"Sonia's mom dumped her idiot boyfriend, so now there's no rush."

"Don't change your plans. It'll only hurt your mother."

"If I left, you wouldn't eat anything but mustard toast."

The corner of one of his eyes twitched. I put my hand on his arm, the way I used to when I was a kid and I wanted to play with his hair. Cindy sent the stroller flying into the ditch and then turned to us, wiping both sides of her hands on her shirt. She started tiptoeing when she saw that I was crying. It was her way of not taking up space. She joined her hands together in prayer, asking forgiveness without knowing what for.

"Are you mad, Lau?"

"'Course not, silly."

She ran to me then, pulling on my clothes as she climbed up my body. When we were at eye level, she buried her cold little nose in my neck.

"They're still moving, ya know…"

"It's not the worms, don't worry."

She pressed her filthy hands against my cheeks. My tears trickled between her fingers, bypassing the knuckles and tracing muddy paths all the way down to her wrists. She wiped them on a pink T-shirt now streaked with brown.

"The strollers was already trashed, Lau…"

"*Were*, not was."

The fact that I was giving her a hard time was a clear sign that I was feeling better. She tilted her head back to show off her teeth, which were growing in crookedly into a snarl no braces could ever fix.

"It's not nice to crush worms like that. They didn't do anything to you."

"They don't even die!"

Worms have more than one heart — I'd learned that when we dissected one in biology class. And they don't have lungs. They breathe through their skin, all over their body. Lucky them.

On the way back, after Cindy had fallen asleep, I moved closer to my father and rested my head on his shoulder. It was the first time I'd ever seen him cry. The pain was stamped in grooves across his forehead. We had just entered a new dimension glazed with immeasurable loss, an afterworld where we would have to learn to live and love each other without her.

15

Ron had closed the garage for the morning, leaving just one guy at the register to take payments for gas. My mother's booth would be ceremoniously torn down by men in clean coveralls. The installation of the electric gate we had all been dreading had turned into a tribute of sorts. When they learned my mother would be leaving, the hospital administration decided to install an automated system. We saw this as a testament of her irreplaceability. After fifteen years of breathing in the dirty parking lot air that had wreaked havoc on her lungs, she deserved the most flattering interpretation.

Before the guys arrived, I moved all her things to my car: the spider plants, the African violets, the Club Med posters in their rolls, the candy jar, the assorted knick-knacks, the space heaters, my graduation picture in its frame, the chamber pot, the books. My father had come by earlier to unscrew the fold-up seat and stool. All that remained was a bunch of boards. I wonder if they retained the echoes of the secrets we'd shared; the salt from my long-dried childhood tears; molecules of skin, clothes, lunches, boredom. My mother had stayed home; she needed to remember her booth as it had been.

"Otherwise it'll get torn down in my memories, too."

The first nails had been yanked out by the time Pichette arrived with enough coffee and doughnuts to go around. Bob pulled out his mulled wine, its flask shiny as a new penny.

"Shoot, did I miss the prayers?"

"What prayers?"

"Aw hell, Pichette. Lay off, will ya?"

Ron was working with a cigarette in his mouth, one eye closed against the white smoke.

"You said we were havin' a funeral for the booth."

"It was a figure of speech."

"Okay, okay! So we're just gonna flatten it?"

Sonia's father's funeral had set off some sort of mystical reckoning for Ron. Seen through the glorifying prism of the priest's words, life had taken on a new meaning for him. He hoped that when his time came, someone would give a eulogy that filled in the cracks and sanded down the prickly edges, and that death would become something more than just a permanent mechanical malfunction. It was almost as if he wanted to die, just to hear his praises sung.

"Go on, Serge, say a few words, will ya?"

"To who?"

"To everybody here."

Parking was free that day. The barrier gate pointed its accusatory arm at the sky, powerless to stop anyone from coming and going. We had never seen so many happy people around the hospital. Visitors lingered, strolled over to their cars, took time to enjoy a cigarette before leaving. Stéphane, the ticket collector with the glass eye, came over to say a few words. When he saw the box of doughnuts, he dived right in. Ron's voice cut through the malaise.

"The rule for a booth is one minute of silence. Say what you gotta say in your head. Go."

Twenty-two seconds later, Bob was back to whistling, crowbar in hand. Once the insulation had been thrown into the dumpster and the boards stacked in the bed of Jingle's pickup (he'd reuse the good ones and build a nice fire with the rest), all that remained of the place was its footprint, along with the debris left by its captives over the seasons. Thousands of years from now, once time had inevitably distorted the facts, future generations might see the medieval ruins as a shrine that immured souls in exchange for divine protection. The mercy of the gods, like parking spots, has always been bought and sold. There's nothing new under the sun.

At the rate my mother was withering away, she would disappear long before she died. An evil force was eating away at her insides. She would wake from her chemical-induced naps only to lose herself in another of her books, nose glued to the pages as she followed the sun from room to room. She was always cold.

"Hey, Mom, we could go to Maine."

"Why?"

"To see the ocean, swim, eat crab cakes."

"Maine is far, sweetheart."

"It's a six-hour drive, a day if we go slow and take lots of breaks. Dad and I could take turns driving."

"Your father would come?"

"We already talked about it. He's game."

"Your father — in the sun?"

"We could set him up under an umbrella, give him a cooler full of beer."

"Oh, Laurie, my love. My baby..."

Her eyes filled with tears that didn't fall, waves suspended in time. She reached out a liver-spotted hand. Soon, Cindy would no longer be able to make silly pictures by connecting the spots like constellations.

"You two are angels, but I'd rather not."

"We'll take really good care of you. We'll bring your medicine and anything else you need…"

"Oh, I'm not worried, honey. Not with you two."

"Then why not?"

"It could never be as beautiful as in my head. I don't have time to be disappointed."

It made sense. Old Orchard Beach could be as breathtaking as the Greek Cyclades as long as they both remained in her imagination. Her dreams formed a free-standing structure that had no use for reality. I think that was the moment I finally understood that the love stories she was so fond of had nothing to do with what my father was, or wasn't.

Soon, Cindy started to notice that nobody was making French toast, pancakes, or maple pudding anymore, and that the fruit bowl wasn't perpetually full. We would have to tell her what was going on. I took her for a walk along the Saint-Charles River, with a lollipop to make the news go down easier. After I had explained the situation using the simplest words I could find, she stared at me for a long while, letting the pieces sink in. I should have known that my imagination, well-oiled as it was, would still leave me unprepared for her reaction.

"Can I brush your teeth, then?"

"My teeth?"

"When you take 'em out."

"But I don't have dentures. These are my real teeth."

"Pff!"

"It's better that way. Suzanne's teeth were all rotten. She had to get them pulled so she could get dentures."

"Why were they rottened?"

"*Rotten*, not rottened."

"You're sooo annoying..."

"Because Suzie never went to the dentist when she was little. Her teeth were full of cavities, and they got bigger as she grew."

"Whatsa dentist?"

The moment we walked into the apartment, she rushed over to my mother to ask where it hurt and where she would go next. The cliché of leaving on a long trip was the best way I could find to explain that, pretty soon, she wouldn't be able to see Suzanne again. Ever. While my mother untangled the mystery of her bodily demise, I went into the kitchen to find the metal cookie tin where she kept all her recipes. I might be able to save one or two while there was still time, as long as I learned all the unwritten tricks that made them so good.

Hélène from bingo came by to drop off a box of good-luck charms that a few of the regulars wanted to pass along. News of my mother's illness had jumped from ear to ear like bionic lice the night I'd run away. When my mother heard her name, she rose to greet the visitor. She wanted to meet the official toilet scrubber in person.

"'Course I remember you, Hélène. The little paper girl. My God, you were such a tiny thing back then..."

"I gave up my route a long time ago."

"Laurie said you have three sisters?"

"Yup. One older and two younger."

"Lucky girl."

"Huh. Not all the time."

My mother flashed me a sideways glance. A wry smile played on her lips. The dark-blue half-moons under her eyes gave them a macabre depth, as if they were sinking back into her head. Hélène lowered her chin slightly.

"Show me whatcha got."

"They're just some silly things, but they're supposed to bring you luck. I dunno if they actually work."

"Can't hurt."

"Fair enough."

There were three rabbits' feet, one hare's foot, a miniature horseshoe, a porcelain cow, a star covered in sequins that were coming unstuck, a baby mitten, a piece of woven palm, and a medal of the Virgin Mary alleged to perform miracles.

"Now you thank everyone for me, will you? Tell them I'm grateful and that I'll keep 'em with me. I'll leave you to it, girls. I have to take a little rest now..."

She'd put all the energy she had into the last few minutes. On her way out, Hélène turned and threw her skinny little arms around me. I wasn't expecting it. A sob rose in my throat.

"I really hope your mom doesn't die."

Her naïveté brought tears to my eyes, and I offered up the truest lie I'd ever told anyone.

"I hope she doesn't, either."

"Think you'll come back to bingo?"

"Yeah, probably, if you haven't found someone else."

"We're splitting your section for now."

"You must be up to your eyeballs."

"It's not so bad, things've been pretty quiet. Plus, we got rid of the ice cream—it was a pain in the ass."

Since my mother was losing strength by the day, Louise insisted on coming by the house to do her dye job. She did house calls for large families—six heads to cut, like over at the Laberges, was worth the trip—and for her elderly clients, who might not receive another visit all month. To return the favour, I picked her up in my Pony and dropped her at the salon afterwards, even though it was only a few blocks away. I was beginning to understand my mother a little better now. Death was an elephant in the room, dwarfing everything around it.

"I sat there with my own mother on her deathbed," Louise told me. "All sixty pounds of her. Kept remindin' us to freshen up her lipstick. Pride never dies, sugar."

"It's so nice of you to come by. I know she really appreciates it."

"I'll do your roots next time, while I'm at it."

"I don't know, I'm thinking about growing it out."

"Oh? No more blond? You make such a nice blonde."

"It's too flashy."

"At your age, you can do flashy."

"I'm not really in the mood."

She laid a hand on my arm. Forty years of chemical rinses and shampoos had done a number on her skin. Beneath the paper-thin layer that remained, blue veins branched out in all directions. I thought about the skeleton-hand symbol on the warning labels of bleach containers.

"Oh, child..."

"It's fine. I'm fine."

"It's okay if you're not."

My father and I were living in a bubble of latent despair, a castle under siege with books for ramparts. We could hold out a little while longer. In the distance, the enemy was chomping at the bit, awaiting the signal

to attack. Sometimes, when we stopped paying attention, their cries would be reduced to background noise.

"I want you to do something for your mom."

"What?"

"You know, we talked a lot over the years."

"I know."

"She just wants you to be happy. It's all she cares
about."

"And that I go to university."

"Same thing. That's one path to happiness."

"I know."

"She won't disown you if you decide not to go."

"How could she? She'll be dead."

In the silence of the car, the roar swelled until it was
deafening: plain speech, stripped of pleasantries, always
cut through the noise. I gripped the steering wheel so I
wouldn't fall to pieces. If I hadn't dropped my classes to
take extra shifts at the restaurant, I would already have
a diploma. Instead, I was watching the days topple like
dominoes and begging all gods known to man to leave
us my mother in exchange for one of the many centen-
arians waiting desperately for death and wondering why
they'd been overlooked. It seemed only right and proper
that a nice lady who'd kept to herself and never made a
fuss, who'd spent her life in a two-bedroom deep in the
outer reaches of the Lower Town, should pass under
the radar.

"Right now, there's just one thing bothering her."

"What's that?"

"That boy you never called back."

"She told you about him?"

"'Course she did. I can keep a secret."

"But it's such awful timing."

"That's what pains her to see. She knows you woulda called him back if it weren't for her, it's eating her up inside."

"What am I supposed to say? 'Hi! Oh, by the way, did I tell you? My mother's dying.'"

She squeezed my arm even harder. The tears were falling again, into a bottomless well. I'd long stopped trying to hide them. She sighed. The rest came bursting out.

"And it's not just that."

"What else is there?"

"It's complicated."

"I'm in no rush."

"I can't."

"You can't tell me?"

"No, I can't... be with a guy like that."

"Is he married? Kids?"

"'Course not, he's twenty-one."

"Fresh outta prison?"

"Pff! Please."

"You laugh, but it happened to me. Dashing young thing, never woulda believed it, so nice, so gentle...

209

And that body, sweet Jesus. With a package like that, we coulda gone all night . . . But he couldn't stay outta trouble . . ."

"He's just a regular student."

"What's he study?"

"Animals."

"Oh! A zoologist!"

"Veterinarian."

"That's what I meant. And where's this regular guy of yours from?"

"Not from around here."

"Ah! I get it . . ."

"What's that mean, 'I get it'?"

"Look at me, sugar."

"Hmm."

"You know exactly what I mean."

Her eyes were drilling a hole through my head; they flashed in understanding. Though I had grown up bathed in my mother's boundless love and admiration, I still hadn't found the strength to love myself unconditionally. What sort of genetic defect could transform such love into self-contempt?

"But now it's too late . . ."

"It's only too late when you're dead, sugar."

. . .

Late the following evening, I pulled up outside Roman's house. Everything was dark, save for the faint glow of sconces lighting the foyer and basement entrances. Mary Poppins was sleeping. Possibly with Jean-Paul. The GTI wasn't in the driveway, of course, since it was still in Charlevoix. I closed my eyes and reached for his neck. *Doo, doo doo, doo doo, doo doo doo doo, doo doo, doo doo ...*

16

My mother knew how to die. Not everyone has such a gift. Her years inside the booth had prepared her well.

Try as she did, it grew harder and harder to ignore the heavy measures she now had to take to keep the pain at bay. We quickly agreed that her medication had to be adjusted: it was impossible to fight an army of evil cells that multiplied exponentially and grew stronger by the hour with a predetermined dosage stamped in ink. We got used to the sound of her books tumbling to the ground, their spines hitting the floor. Cheap paperbacks would split apart almost immediately, prompting me to reinforce their covers with multiple layers of clear packing tape. It gave their spines a new lustre. The library didn't seem to mind.

The day that *Love in the Time of Cholera* hit the floor-boards, I abandoned the cup of butter I'd left sitting out at room temperature in preparation for the apple crisp ("not too soft, or it'll melt into the oatmeal and you'll lose the crispness") and went to rescue the book from where it lay on the floor, out of reach of my mother's defeated hand. We upped the painkillers, fluffed the pillows, and adjusted the headrests, convinced that comfort was somehow still achievable. I sat down beside my mother on the rusty latched steamer trunk handed down from her father, who was long dead by the time I was born. I waited until peace had settled over her face before opening the book to the most recent dog-eared page. We'd start from there. I would read the first half during her naps. By taking the numbers meticulously recorded on the fly-leaf and multiplying them by a coefficient devised to account for the slower pace of reading out loud, I could make my mother a personalized travel schedule. A little like Nelson Mandela, or history's other great recluses.

We floated off to the Caribbean on the strange bubble of my voice, a magic carpet ride of sorts, and we stayed there quite a while — thirteen hours and forty-five minutes spread over five days, the length of a love affair spanning fifty-three years, seven months, and eleven days and nights. We carved out an existence in the belly of a Russian doll where time expanded as the chapters flew by. In the world of the living, it would have taken months to rack up so much time spent together. This life on the fringes of reality afforded us a few extra years. It was our way of thumbing our noses at her disease's rapid advance.

After spending the first few days whining, Cindy had come to appreciate how my voice, like the white noise of a fan, knocked her out after a few pages. She would rather listen than do homework or study. The stories I read were set in places we had already "visited," or that we conjured up on the fly to bring them to life. People lived there, people who weren't us; that was enough. Whenever my mother fell asleep before Cindy did, we'd take a ride in the Pony. Little by little, I was surrendering it to the cancer that was eating away at its parts. The solution to every problem seemed to involve spending money, and I had swapped money for time. Time with her.

So that my father wouldn't feel cast aside, we'd devised a plan he was unlikely to ever suspect: when we knew he was within earshot and liable to listen in, despite himself — he usually found our novels overly complex and too full of characters — I would put aside the book we were working on and pick up another we read at the same time. I began with *The Old Man and the Sea*. When I could feel my father's ears on me, I would pick up the Hemingway where I had left off.

He never guessed that I had changed books, figuring instead that he had missed out on a few long, unnecessary digressions, which is what he thought all books were filled with, anyway. On the third day at sea, when the exhausted old fisherman is ready to drop, his hand mangled from holding the line taut, I could feel my father pause in the living room. He sat there almost motionless. There was no television, no radio. When the sharks finished off the last of the marlin, he rose with a sigh and the heavy step of a fisherman who has just lost everything.

I did the same thing with a collection of short stories by Philip K. Dick, whom I'd just discovered in my literature class. To throw him off, just a little. After that, he started reading the titles of the books we left around the house. My mother got a kick out of the whole thing.

The words had a different taste when I read them aloud. It was like another language, more acrobatic and demanding. A few hours of physically exerting my mouth filled me with a jubilation that was hard to describe. That summer afforded me the leisure to lose myself at my mother's side in the pages that became the fragile sanctuary of our fight against death.

It was a cool, rainy evening. Sonia and I were on Rue Saint-Jean, where the street lights cast yellowish halos through the mist. In one soggy gust, the wind tore through the blow-out Louise had given me as a pick-me-up. When I caught my reflection in the window of a bookstore, my arms dangling awkwardly by my sides, I wondered what I was even doing there, pretending to be enjoying myself. It might not have been impossible, if I had had a spare brain. The window display featured colourful umbrellas and plastic buckets to promote the summer's hottest beach reads.

The kamikazes Sonia and I had put away at Bar Sainte-Angèle had done little other than leave our breath laced with artificial lime. We had vague plans to go dancing somewhere on Grande-Allée and maybe grab a frosty from Wendy's on the way if it was still open. All I really wanted to do was jump on the first bus I could find in Place d'Youville and ride it all the way down the hill home. But I'd make an effort for Sonia. She only wanted the best for me.

Across the street and a few doors down I saw Roman stepping out of Le D'Auteuil with a group of friends. A cloud of blue smoke and jazz slipped out the door with them.

"Sonia! Shit! It's Roman!"

"Where where where?"

"There! In the white polo shirt. Holding the door."

"*Your* Roman?"

"Don't move, or he'll see us."

"You said he was just 'okay,' but he looks cute from here. Some girl's holding his arm. I'm gonna go kick the shit outta her."

"Don't you dare."

She sprinted across the street without a backward glance, leaving me no time to shout or hold her back. The scene unfolded in a sequence of silent frames. Roman looked surprised as Sonia approached. I could tell by the way his eyebrows furrowed. Then he reached out a hand and flashed a smile: beautiful teeth, two dimples. He hunched his shoulders slightly and lowered himself a few inches as I imagined he would do to speak to a child. Sonia pointed at me, and I saw Roman's eyes follow her finger. Eyebrows unfurrowed. There I stood across the street, petrified, a pillar of salt surrounded by warm bodies in motion. I could hear the blood pounding in my temples. Sonia came back over to me, skipping like a child.

"He's even cuter when he talks! I *knew* it was a good idea to go out!"

The people Roman was with started walking down the street away from us. The girl holding on to Roman's arm tried to pull him along. It was hard to say from here whether she was pretty. She couldn't be the jellyfish from the party, she wasn't luminescent enough. He shook his head at her, *no*. She let her hand fall from his arm, as if the thread holding her to him had just been cut, put her hands on her hips, and stuck out her chin. Another finger, Roman's this time, was pointing at me. The girl looked in my direction, tossed her head, and turned to follow the others.

"She's not his girlfriend."

"You asked him?"

"No, but I could tell."

"I didn't realize you were a mind-reader now, JoJo Savard..."

"He's got the face of a redhead, it's adorable..."

"Shh! He's coming over."

"Oh! I need to pee, I'm going over to McDonald's. See you later! Or not."

"Wait for me!"

"NO! I wanna pee alone."

She took off at a run in the opposite direction, just as Roman stepped onto my sidewalk. It all looked so juvenile. To add a touch of comedy, the drizzle had turned to steady rain. Beads of water fell onto his hair, licked his forehead and formed a pool on his eyebrows before launching themselves back into the night air. The most reckless leaped right off his nose. His freckles looked darker, more defined. Cuter. As we moved towards one another, closing the gap and soaked, passersby were forced to sidestep us in one fluid motion.

"Hey."

"Hi."

"Did I scare your friend away?"

"No, she had to pee."

"Rain looks good on you."

His mouth hung open on the last syllable, his lips parted in midair. In the moment, I couldn't imagine why I hadn't tasted them before.

"I look like a mop."

"You look like a girl from a tornado movie."

"Uh...thanks."

"Any time."

"What're you doing in the city?"

"I'm off for three days."

"How's the internship going?"

"Large animals are tough to work with."

"You said that about small ones, too."

"The small ones aren't as messy, but their owners are more annoying."

"Go for medium-sized ones then."

"I was thinking taxidermy."

"That gets awfully dusty."

"Nothing's perfect. How're things with you?"

"In general, or right now?"

"Uh...in general?"

I gave a little noncommittal nod so I wouldn't have to lie.

"No? Okay. Anything to do with how you never called me back?"

"A little."

"Okay. And how're things right now?"

"Better than before."

His friends were still in sight, but they were blurry little stick figures in the distance.

"Your friends are leaving."

"My God! Bye!"

He took off like Roadrunner, elbows and knees pumping at right angles all the way to the corner. As he ran, he kicked up splashes of dirty water that lashed his back. Then he rushed right back, index finger in the air and mouth open, water slipping in from all angles.

"So, Laurie, I was wondering... are you busy? Like, right now?"

"Not really. But you'll lose your friends."

"Meh! I have others."

"I have to tell you something."

His finger fell into place with the others. He was serious now.

"I... it's hard to explain... I was feeling fine at the party, I made the whole sickness thing up... I just couldn't do it, with all the ivy and everything... it looked too much like a castle. And the girls, especially the girls, with their clothes, their rings, their teeth— mine are all crooked, my eye teeth are too squished together—I like hands, I always notice other people's hands...Sonia would kill me if she heard me say that. I know it's weird, but...I was picturing myself holding a wine glass and I knew I'd mess it up...The same thing happens with the faucets in Chem class...some people can't figure out how to turn them on, even though they're just regular faucets...they're the same kind as kitchen faucets, only they're in a lab...Sometimes my brain just can't process it...I could've just grabbed a beer, they're easier—there's no wrong way to hold a beer, really—but they're less classy...for starters, they're brown...I just didn't have the guts to go in, and then the girl called me 'the girl from the garage' and I felt stupid, so I left...And then I felt dumb for lying about being sick, but I didn't know how to tell you I'd made the whole thing up so I could get away without looking crazy...I really wanted to see you that night, but somehow I kept wondering...because it's true, really...I was wondering...well, why aren't you going out with one of those girls?"

"Wow! I think you need to come up for some air!"

"Pff..."

"You want to know why?"

"Uh-huh."

"Because half of those girls are already dating my friends..."

"Oh..."

"...and the other half aren't funny."

His eyes were laughing. In their corners, I could already see the crow's feet that would bloom there one day.

"The thing is, I met you at a garage. If I'd met you in a grocery store, I would have called you 'the girl from the grocery store.' Or 'the girl from the bakery,' if I'd met you there. Or 'the girl from the hardware store...'"

"I get the idea."

He shrugged apologetically and tilted his head forty-five degrees.

"Can I ask you something?"

"Uh-huh."

"Would you ... be interested in a cat?"

"A cat? Jean-Paul?"

"No! My mother would never get over it. A different cat."

"How many legs?"

"Four, for the moment. But no tail."

"No tail?"

"It's not a big deal, he doesn't need it. He's super cute, anyway. Cats aren't like people in that respect."

"Another harvester thingy?"

"Nope. Car door."

"Poor little guy!"

"He's actually pretty big."

"Did he make a full recovery?"

"Physically, yes. Psychologically, it's a different story."

"He must be scared of cars."

"No, that's not it . . . He thinks he's a lizard and that it'll grow back."

"Personality disorder."

"Exactly. What do you think? Sweet, no?"

"I'll ask my parents and get back to you."

"I can take care of his checkups."

"Good thing."

"He's still on the farm. I'll bring him back the next time I'm home."

"What's his name?"

"Whatever you want."

"Is that all one word?"

His teeth really were beautiful. My nipples hardened under my T-shirt, which the rain had rendered see-through. I pinched the fabric around my belly button and tugged to unstick it. No luck; the shirt clung to me even closer than before.

"Are you cold?"

"A little."

Sonia ran past on the opposite side of the street, one hand giving a thumbs up, the other covering her head. She didn't even slow down.

"Isn't that your friend Sonia?"

"Looks like it."

"Maybe she couldn't find a bathroom."

"Pff . . ."

"Want to grab a taxi with me?"

"And go where?"

"Anywhere there's a dryer."

"You mean like a laundromat?"

"The problem is that we don't have a change of clothes to wear while we're waiting for our stuff to dry."

"Good point."

"My place isn't as exotic as the wash and fold, but we do have bathrobes."

"And blue wine."

Our faces were scarcely two inches apart. He slipped a hand into the space and placed it on my cheek.

"Is it dangerous to kiss someone with crooked eye teeth?"

"Not that I'm aware of."

"Dad?"

"Hmm?"

"Don't wait up for me. I might not be home tonight."

"Everything okay?"

"I'm with Roman."

"Who's that?"

"The boy with the GTI."

"Oh! Hang on, your mother's talking to me..."

"She isn't sleeping?"

"'Course not, you know her. Hang on... Okay, yeah... She says she feels better today. Stay out as long as you like, she says she's fine."

Jean-Paul found the patch of sunlight that had just pierced through the clouds and curled up like a hairy snail in the space between our intertwined legs. Our wet clothes were lying in a smelly ball just out of reach.

17

"I started to worry, seeing as she hadn't come by in three days. Your father went to go check..."

"Check what?"

She held her chin to stop it from shaking. On the living-room table, baby spider plants were trying to grow new roots in glasses of murky water. Those that didn't succeed would die upright.

"They're gone, darling..."

"Who is? Gone where?"

"Cindy. They're gone, sweetheart."

"What do you mean, they're gone? How?"

"They moved."

"Where?"

"We don't know."

"Oh, come on, people don't just disappear like that!"

"The apartment was full of junk. No furniture, no people, nothing."

"Someone must have seen them go?"

"Your father says no."

"They can't have gone far; her dad works down the street."

"Your father dropped by the Sunoco..."

"And?"

"He hasn't worked there for two weeks."

"What do you mean?"

"He was stealing from the cash."

"Bastard!"

"He's a broken man."

"They probably just went to the next town over. The landlord must know."

"They made a run for it in the middle of the night. Hadn't paid the rent in three months."

"Fuck!"

I didn't wait to hear more. I slammed the door and ran. A car screeched to a stop inches from my knees, and the driver called me a crazy bitch. The smell of burnt rubber and gravel rose from the pavement. I flew into a rage and took it out on his bumper. A gift from the crazy bitch.

The door wasn't locked. A small man with stooped shoulders was sweeping piles of trash into one giant heap in the centre of the room, forming a mountain of dirty dishes, old clothes, and bits of broken furniture. Shreds of an existence. The smell was unbearable. He put everything into heavy-duty burlap bags that he stacked in the corners to distribute the weight.

"Where'd they go?"

"Beats me, but if I find out I'll have 'em skinned alive, the bastards. Look at this place! Buncha filthy animals..."

"They left all their stuff behind?"

"You don't have time to take much when you bolt like a dog...I dunno how they could live in such a dump...with a kid, too, boggles the mind...they owe three months' rent, besides! I thought about draggin' the sons 'a bitches to the Rental Board...And that ain't the half of it—they clogged the toilet on purpose. Might as well sell the place, for all the trouble it's worth...I'm the one stuck cleanin' up after them pieces of shit... Rent ain't free, no sir, someone's gotta pay, an' this is the thanks I get for puttin' a roof over their heads..."

Beside the door, one of the shoes Cindy often stole from her mother was playing dead, its heel dangling by a thread. I rummaged through the rubble for its match.

And I ran to her school. The yard was packed with children playing hopscotch, dodgeball, or nothing at all. A group of boys was off in one corner making trouble, for fun or for real I couldn't tell; here and there little clusters of girls were scheming up tricks to play on the boys they claimed to hate but really liked; a little further on, the usual outcasts were gripping the chain-link fence and kicking loose pieces of asphalt. A woman approached me with an eyebrow raised and one hand holding the back of her neck.

"Can I help you?"

"I'm looking for a little girl named Cindy."

"Who are you?"

"A friend."

"You're a little old to be a friend."

"A friend of the family."

"What's this about?"

"I just came to see her. I want to talk to her."

"Is it important?"

"No. Can't I just see her for thirty seconds?"

"We try to protect the children, miss. There are some twisted people out there who can't wait to get their hands on a little kid."

"I know."

"What's Cindy's last name?"

"Leclerc."

"And what grade is she in?"

"Grade two."

"I'll go ask. I'm just the monitor, I don't know everyone's name."

I kept seeing Cindy everywhere, in each skinny little girl who passed by. She would dissolve the moment I caught sight of a too-small nose, too-big eyes, an obedient smile.

Everyone the monitor asked shook their head from side to side. Nobody knew anything. I hung around so as not to look like a creep, and to stay on her good side in case I had to return. A different woman came to find me, one with purpose in her step and the eyes of a saviour.

"Hello."

"Hello."

"Are you the one looking for Cindy Leclerc?"

"Yes."

"She's been absent for a week now."

"Are you her teacher?"

"Yes."

"They moved."

"Oh? Where to?"

"I don't know, that's why I came by. I'm looking for her. There's nobody at her house."

"As far as I know, her file hasn't been transferred to another school."

"She's not going to school?"

"It's hard to say. Sometimes the transfer takes a while, and there isn't much follow-up."

"What can we do?"

"Not much, unfortunately."

"But isn't school mandatory?"

"Yes, but we don't have the resources to chase down

every case. I'll put a note in her file that they've moved, like you said. That's something, at least."

She shot me a sad smile that spoke volumes about the coexistence of real and imaginary worlds, about the underfed little girls who fall through the cracks of a vast system.

"What's your name?"

"Laurie."

"I'm Clara."

A name suffused with wildflowers that perfumed the countryside. She went back to trying to save the others.

I passed by the garage on my way home.

"My dad isn't back yet?"

"Nah, he's still out looking. Pichette and Jingle are off somewhere out by Saint-Albert."

"Okay, cool."

"We radioed in, sent some other guys out looking, too. Gotta get 'em off their asses for once, buncha slackers!"

"They won't find her..."

"Your father finds everything."

Ron started hacking up a lung, shoulders shaking under the force of it. He sounded like a muffler that was cracked from end to end, catalytic converter and all. With all the coughing, he must have had abs of steel.

"You should go see a doctor."

"I smoke two packs a day."

"So?"

"They'll tell me to stop."

"Then stop."

"I can't."

"Why not?"

"It makes me wanna kill people."

He laid the power screwdriver on the hood of the car and grabbed a rag that was too dirty to clean a thing. The noise of all we would leave unsaid echoed throughout the garage. I got the impression he would have wrapped me in his arms if he'd known how. The chimes of the food truck floated towards us in tinny spirals.

"Come on, coffee's on me."

"I can't, I don't have time."

"Sure you do. They'll find your lil' fleabag. People like that never make it very far, just move from one shithole to the next. Bob has five bucks on the guys findin' her before four o'clock."

"Do you still have that crazy glue?"

"You can't glue a muffler."

"It's not for my muffler."

"Bring 'er in, we'll fix 'er up. Don't want the cops pullin' you over."

"It's just for this."

I showed him the broken shoe.

. . .

We couldn't bring ourselves to open a book. We were wholly consumed by the wait. I would have gone out in the Pony, but I couldn't leave my mother alone. It would have helped to believe in something, to improvise a makeshift god for the occasion. But we couldn't. Our shaky faith crumbled under the weight of our hope, and the thought of never seeing Cindy again pummeled us at every turn. What if she never came back...

"You were right, sweetie, we should adopt her. It'd be better."

Very slowly, my mother turned to me. She was smiling. This was it.

"Her parents wouldn't have to know."

"She wouldn't, either."

"You two are already like sisters."

"True. She takes my things, gets on my nerves..."

"We might need a certificate."

"I'm on it. I still have that fountain pen you and Dad gave me for my birthday."

"We could make some egg sandwiches to celebrate. She'd be so tickled."

"With extra mayo."

"And grape juice. But we ran out of straws, you know she loves them."

"Don't worry, Mom. I'll go pick some up."

Ceremonies require some pomp and circumstance. We weren't about to do things by halves.

Bob lost his five bucks. The men didn't come back until dinnertime. My mother was dozing by the time I heard footsteps on the wrought-iron staircase outside. A filthy little hand appeared in the window of the door, and then a tuft of hair. My father and Pichette followed behind her, caps in hands, like at church. Somehow, my weak knees managed to bear my weight. My mother sat up. I was able to hide the trembling in my voice.

"Hey, kid!"

We tried to act as if we weren't climbing out from a pit of quicksand.

"Hey, fatass!"

She ran to me, stuck her cold little nose into the crook of my neck, and sighed. I closed my eyes and breathed in the smell of her dusty head. My mother ran a skeletal hand through her hair, a comb of flesh and bone.

"My, that hair grows fast!"

"Pff."

"What's all this about moving?"

"I hate the new place. It's gross."

"It can't be that bad..."

"It smells."

"What does it smell like?"

"Ass."

"Cindy! Watch your language."

"My mom's the one who said it!"

"Are you hungry?"

"Yeah."

"Would you like an egg sandwich?"

"Yeaaah!"

In the end, the victory had gone to Pichette. He'd found her searching for loose change in a phone booth. Someone had wisely suggested they check the convenience stores, those watering holes of parched souls everywhere. I wanted to show my gratitude without giving her false hope, so I handed her a sandwich bun stuffed to the brim.

"Cindy, look what I have for you."

"What?"

"Over there, on the ground."

"My shoes! You found 'em! They were all busted up!"

I thought: adoption gift. We toasted with grape Crush drunk through red-and-white-striped bendable straws.

We took my father's shortcut through Cartier-Brébeuf Park, and ten minutes later we were standing beside the staircase that led to the semi-basement they now occupied. Dirty, ugly grey—from the outside, it was utterly depressing. A real shithole. Only thing missing was the railroad tracks.

"Will you remember the way?"

"Nope."

"Seriously? You didn't pay attention on the walk over?"

"I like it better when you come git me."

"*Get*. When you come *get* me."

"Aah! You're sooo annoying!"

"Okay, we'll meet in the park until you can learn the way."

"When?"

"How about after school? You're still going to school, right?"

"I don't gotta choice, or the cops'll come after me..."

As she walked, she stepped on the hems of her pants, which were coming apart in muddy threads. The jeans had slipped down over her narrow hips, putting the top of her little bum on full display. I'd have to find her a belt. I'd somehow convinced her to leave the high heels at home so they wouldn't break. In this half-formed little girl, wobbling away on a shaky foundation, we had found the ideal recipient for my mother's excess love. We had carved out a place for her in our family, and she had captured our hearts. Forever. From now on, it would be up to me. Good thing I had love of my own to spare.

. . .

The Pony died a few days later. Fittingly, its heart gave out as we climbed Côte d'Abraham, headed towards Upper Town. If you're going to die, might as well do it with panache, on a road steeped in history and ghosts. It makes for a better story later on down the line.

For two weeks, I'd been ignoring the "check engine" light on the dash, hoping it was a minor problem or a wiring issue that could wait. But, as my father had taught me even before I learned my ABCs, when an engine is low on oil, irritation can quickly spill over into a mutinous rage. What remains of the wreckage can be tough to get back on track. I gave the Pony to Pichette when he came to tow us away. In his spare time, he might be able to rescue it, with enough love. Nobody else would, that much I knew.

My mother had heard the whole story before I even got home, thanks to the all-knowing softies on the two-way. I'd hit a low wall when I tried to pull over too quickly, and my hip and my collarbone had taken the brunt of the impact from the seat belt, just as the South Koreans who built my car intended. No matter how many times she'd been assured I wasn't hurt, she didn't unclench her teeth until she saw me standing in front of her, all in one piece. Her face relaxed, her body continued its dying. Two words were enough to sum up all she had to say.

"Goddamn cars..."

It was our last good laugh.

It wasn't yet November, month of the dead, when a spiral of complications forced us to transfer my mother to the hospital. We knew all too well that this time she wouldn't be coming back. Swaddled like a newborn in the blankets we used to play "cabin," she let her eyes slip one last time over the backdrop of her physical life through a blur of resigned tears. There would be no more late nights out on the stoop, no more neighbourly hellos marked by a nod, no more children shouting in the alley, no more stones kicked down the sidewalk, no more fragrant breezes. She would never again look up to see the sky over her head. Now, the constellations would be formed out of tubes and wires against a ceiling pocked by rings of moisture. She knew how to withdraw to sweeter places, that part didn't scare her. But, oh, the sounds of living things...

18

Time had become a formless goo gumming up the works and mechanisms that once lent order to our lives. We were living in a world of melting timepieces, hurtling over rapids with our hands tied behind our backs, coming up for air between waves, not knowing if we would be swept away by the roar or overpowered by the water.

I spent as much time with my mother as the hospital would allow. Even when she was high on morphine, floating in a body so withered it no longer left an impression in the mattress, I would lean over close and whisper the words of her favourite novels in her ear. The doctors said she could still hear. It was their way of easing *my* pain, of caring for me as best they could. She was on the

floor of the doomed. Patients either arrived holding flowers or were minutes away from receiving them. Everyone
who set foot there died a little bit. Overwhelmed by the
pain, my father crumpled into the armchair in the corner,
his hands filling the grooves of the worn wood that had
cradled so many bodies before him.

"I brought *The Thorn Birds.*"

"Oh, my! That's a good . . . fifteen hours. More, even,
if you read aloud . . ."

"We have time."

"What about school?"

"I'm going, Mom. I just have to take the two courses
I dropped last winter, and then I'm done."

"Promise me you'll finish?"

"I promise."

"I'll never see your diploma . . ."

"It's just a regular piece of paper. Only thicker."

"Still . . ."

"I'm going to get it, Mom. And lots more after."

"I know, baby, I know. You work so hard . . ."

"Just like you."

"Eh, I'm not winning any prizes these days."

"Pff . . ."

I could tell from her eyes brimming with happiness
that she was imagining a beautiful graduation ceremony
for me. Like everything now, it was a thousand miles
from reality.

"I could just read the best parts, if you prefer."

"Now that's an idea..."

"The ones with Father de Bricassart."

"Bah..."

"What?"

The air and bed were like a vise slowly tightening around her body, day by day. The words crawled up from besieged lungs into her throat, then slipped out between her lips.

"The coward..."

"That heartthrob Ralph?"

"Money...the church...gimme sheep any day."

We had never really talked about the books we read on our own. I must have seen her pick this one up a hundred times, never stopping to wonder what she saw in it, what need it filled, what escape it provided. I felt suddenly dizzy from all the questions I'd never be able to ask her.

Sonia came by to boost my morale between her classes and shifts at The Bay. She spent her days folding pyjamas, clipping large panties onto plastic hangers, and pointing customers to the right aisles and sizes, the best bang for their buck. For my benefit, she concocted imaginary scenarios featuring bewildered men searching the lingerie section for sexy negligees. She was having an affair with James, the Anglo from the electronics department. We broke out our best garage talk using buttons, remote controls, and all manner of switches as metaphors. Presumably, the guy was better with machines.

"You're so skinny, Lau. It's scary."

"You're just worried I'll look better in a bikini."

"I'm worried you'll fall through the next storm drain you come across. Eat this."

Two ultra-crispy corn dogs topped with ballpark mustard. The girl really loved me.

"And you don't get out enough. You're as pasty as the walls."

"I know. But it could happen tomorrow, or...any minute."

"I know."

And nobody knew better than she did. She really missed her stubborn old father and would have given anything just to hold his hand until the end, together in the rowboat.

One of the librarians came by the house to drop off the very first available copy of *The Bridges of Madison County*. She knew about my mother and didn't want her to lose her spot on the reservation list, which was over two pages long. If she didn't check it out now, it might be too late.

Intrigued by this novella that was flying off the shelves of American booksellers, I opened it with the intention of reading a few pages before bed. I wanted to picture the flat Iowa landscape that, on the journey from English to French, had somehow lost its bridges to become *Sur la route de Madison*. When Robert Kincaid walked into Francesca's ordinary kitchen with his beer cans and hippie grin and saw her, an equally ordinary mother in her mid-forties — when I realized that this time, the love story would not unfold against the exotic backdrop my mother had become so used to imagining for herself — I wondered if her heart, battered by illness, could bear to see itself painted in such unsparing light, without the artifice of the usual shock-absorbers.

"She's Italian?"

"Yes, but her husband brought her to the United States after the war."

"Right, that explains the dark hair..."

"Yeah."

"And they dance?"

"In the kitchen, yes. And listen to the radio."

"Oh! The radio..."

"A commercial comes on right when they start dancing, so they have to wait for the next song. It's a little awkward."

"Mmm..."

"But it's just the two of them."

"..."

"I'll start from the beginning, when the photographer arrives, okay?"

"Oh, yes..."

The nurse looked at me tenderly. I had been reading the same scene over and over for the past two days. My mother seemed perpetually confused: snowy plains, cotton fields, and Irish steppes blended together to occupy the same space in her mind, where characters out of her own thousand and one nights roamed. She listened with eyes wide open, as if the action were playing out for her on the ceiling.

"Kincaid asks her to come with him."

"..."

"He wants her to leave everything behind and follow him."

"..."

"But there's her husband. He's kinda boring, but he's a decent guy. And her kids."

"..."

"Francesca is desperately in love with him..."

"..."

My mother never found out that Francesca didn't go with Kincaid, not even after spending the best days of her life with him. But it didn't matter. She would have written that part of the story in exactly the same way if someone had asked her to. Like Francesca, if she had been given the chance to take off with the man of her dreams, she would have chosen my father and me. There was something comforting about this bittersweet ending: my mother might very well have had a secret lover who'd given her the strength to stay with us. The fact that she chose to remain by our sides said nothing of her secret lives, nor of her love for my father, which may never have faltered, for that matter. The beauty of it lay in the myriad possibilities. And I liked to think that she died dancing in a kitchen with a yellow Formica table. Ours was off-white, but I bet she could have worked something out.

I opened the book to the flyleaf and wrote: *November 15–18, 1993.*

19

"Suzanne would have loved to see you gathered here together today...in the house of the Lord, our Lord... our guide...to walk with her and say a final goodbye before setting off on the ultimate adventure...Suzanne had a passion for life and was always quick with a kind word...she was a lifelong lover of books who went to be with the Lord, who left this world doing what she loved most...Suzanne is now living out her dreams for all eternity, may she rest in peace..."

The priest was tipsy. Everyone sitting in the first row of pews could see the swaying, notice the clipped movements. Oft-repeated stock phrases sapped the meaning from his eulogy, and we took this as permission to zone out every now and then. For us, at any rate, the real ceremony had unfolded elsewhere, in the privacy of our apartment, alive with familiar smells and genuine images. This one was for everyone else, for anyone who needed an intermediary and an official rite to accept death. I leaned against my father's shoulder and took his gnarled hand in mine. Roman was a sturdy presence, quietly holding my arm on the other side. There was no way I could fall. Behind me, in my shadow, Sonia kept blowing her nose. As a precaution, we had kept Cindy away from all of this, as much for her sake as her parents'. Though I had bought her a new dress, on principle. Within an hour, she had torn the collar "by assident."

"... she was a loving wife and mother that God has called back home... surrounded in life, as in death, by a devoted circle of friends..."

Looking solemn in his church clothes, Pichette ducked into the second row and sat down beside the Lake Country cousins. He tried desperately to keep up with the responsive reading, knelt and rose a half-second behind the rest of the congregation, tripped over the kneeler, fidgeted compulsively with his tie. Seeing his chest swell in time with the organ, you would have thought he was plugged into its pipes. Unfortunately for him, he was too late; the churches had already begun purging their walls of splashy paraphernalia in an effort to restore life to sanctuaries empty of faith.

The guys were waiting for communion outside in the snow, flasks of gin in hand. From the mouths of the damned swirled clouds of cigarette smoke, misty breath, and tiny droplets of alcohol that hung in the air. Nobody felt like laughing; instead, they drank copiously. The cold numbed the rest.

They were still waiting to be called in when the priest, who had been trying to skirt the enormous wooden nativity scene installed in the sacristy, caught his chasuble on a tine of the shepherd's pitchfork — a tool everyone believed to be decorative, and therefore harmless. Too focused on keeping his eyes straight ahead, the priest kept walking until the pitchfork lodged itself in the altar rail, causing the man to plunge head first down the three steps that led to the sinners' nave. His body went slack; his swollen fingers made no attempt to break his fall, contrary to instinct. The chalice went flying, tracing an ellipsis through the air and releasing the hosts in a beautiful white arc before scattering them onto the soggy floor. The poor man's head struck the terrazzo without so much as a fight. *Oh!*s and *Ah!*s of consternation echoed throughout the church. The first mourners to rush over stepped into a small puddle of blood that had begun pooling around the point of contact.

"Don't touch him!"

"Turn him over! We can't just leave him like that!"

"What if he broke his neck? Better wait for the ambulance."

"CALL AN AMBULANCE!"

"He's alive! I can hear him moaning!"

The priest mumbled something unintelligible.

"CAN YOU HEAR US, FATHER?"

"Arghdontshoutlikethatpfffffortheluvvagod..."

One of his arms came back to life, and he managed to prop himself up before finding the energy to push himself onto his back.

"My God! Look at his face!"

There was blood everywhere: it looked like he was sweating it out of his pores.

"WATER! WATER!"

A man I didn't know grabbed his wife's scarf — he wasn't wearing one — and ran to dip it into the holy water. After wringing it out over the priest's face, once and then twice, it became clear that the blood was coming from his right eyebrow. The flesh closed around the wound in little apricot-coloured puckers that materialized as the water fell.

While the church warden tried to gather the hosts that hadn't been swallowed by the slush, the paramedics wrapped up the drunken priest. He had given up the fight against his inebriety and was laughing freely. Luckily, the paramedic with the scar wasn't on duty. His beauty had no place in this pathetic scene.

The bereaved who were worried that skipping communion during a mass—a funeral mass, at that—might slow their ascension to the pearly gates literally threw themselves onto the sandwiches being served in the basement: some joker who enjoyed a good prank had convinced the crowd the sandwiches had been blessed, along with the hosts, through some form of divine ricochet effect. A wafer for the price of an egg salad. At least the sandwiches weren't dyed blue this time. For weeks to come, the guys from the pit would spin the accident every which way—it didn't matter that they had missed the main event—until it became a whale of a tale. Their story began as the mass opened, with a few gulps of sacramental wine drunk in secret while the organ shrieked to wake the dead. It ended with the priest's spectacular wipeout, noting that his brains had come within an inch of painting the floor. Pichette didn't laugh as much as the others.

The girls from the bakery had come to pay their respects, decked out as bridesmaids with wedding-cake hair. Had I gotten married, they couldn't have done more, save swap out the black for mint green. Lise smelled like fresh bread. I cried like a baby when she wrapped me in her arms.

Estelle had also made the trip. She had aged almost overnight, like Dorian Gray before his portrait. What remained of her body, once the restaurants had sucked all the youth from it, nobody wanted. Her days consisted of long battles with boredom, which she lost more often than not. She didn't like seniors' clubs, or bingo, or reading. "I'm getting along just fine, doll, don't you worry 'bout me." But I worried, anyway, for a good long while.

Claude, wherever he was, had sent the beautiful flowering peace lily we placed next to the urn. I scanned the crowd but didn't find him, then turned my eyes to the sky, home of the omniscient. It was the only potted plant we received. I took it home and kept it.

Since the law prohibited spreading the ashes of loved ones wherever we wanted, I kept a low profile. I took a few spoonfuls of my mother, safely tucked away in the urn of books we had created for her, and put them into a paper bag. In the hospital parking lot, I stood on the concrete base of the electronic barrier and clipped one of the bag's corners. I put a hand underneath the spout to catch a bit of my mother as the powder rushed out. When I blew on it, some bits of her flew into the air, others mixed in with the snowflakes that had fallen hours earlier, and the rest remained trapped in the lines of my palm, forming a tree of dark, slender branches. It didn't matter where she ended up; her resting place was purely symbolic. She hadn't obeyed the laws of physics when she was alive. Death wouldn't be any different.

20

"Look! Lookit this!"

"Hang on, let me get there first."

Cindy often pouted as she waited for me at the bus stop. There were days I came home late from class, or not at all, so she would get pre-emptively mad at me, just in case. If she worked herself up, she wouldn't be as disappointed.

"What is it?"

"Look closer!"

A loose-leaf page smudged with scribbles and greyish eraser smears, with a "7/10" circled in red. In the upper left-hand corner, her name in capital letters. Instead of a dot, there was a dark cloud over the *i*. Only idiots dotted their *i*s with hearts, duh. I'd been an idiot at her age.

"Seven out of ten? What happened?"

"I dunno."

"You studied, kiddo! That's the key. And look where it got you! Wow!"

"Think I kin be a hairdresser now?"

"If you keep this up, absolutely. You can be anything you want."

Every time she had a reason to be proud of herself, she bit her fingernails. She dreamed of having a salon like Louise's, with shelves filled with products to mix special colours and a shower head at the end of a long hose she could use to clean the floors, take a shower in the middle of the salon, and water the plants (or hose down anyone who tried to steal). Oh, and to wash hair.

"Don't do that, your hands are filthy!"

"I wanna surprise."

"It isn't polite to ask. I tell you that all the time."

"But you won't gimme one if I don't!"

"Do you really think I'd ignore a seven out of ten?"

"Nah."

"You know you shouldn't ask. Come on, let's go home."

"Bobolink's there."

Before introducing Roman to Cindy, I'd suggested that he give her something to eat as a peace offering. The result was predictable: she liked him "a little." Because I liked him a little too much.

"With Serge?"

"They're doin' something with the car."

"They have to change a few parts. Suzie didn't follow you?"

"Nah, he's eating a bird."

When it came time to name the tailless cat, Cindy had suggested *Suzie*. My father didn't say no, but he found it a little twisted, especially since the cat was a male. To him, it was The Cat; to her, it was Suzie; to Roman and me, Whateveryouwant.

"Another one? What kind?"

"Sparra."

"*Sparrow*."

"You're sooo annoying!"

Once we rounded the bend in the alley, we could see two sets of legs sticking out from under the car, like corpses. Roman wanted to watch my father tinker so he could pick up a little automobile medicine, and my father took the opportunity to guide a pair of young, undamaged hands. Bottles of beer waited patiently on the hood. They would drink it lukewarm, once again, and act as if it'd come right out of the fridge. Roman might play a little guitar, possibly even the song Cindy loved with all the *doo, doo doo, doo doo, doo doo doo doo, doo doos*...

Ron didn't make it through the winter. All the hacking up a lung had hacked a hole clear through, and death slipped in unannounced, like the coward it always is. We held the ceremony in the garage. Only close friends and family. Pichette gave an emotional eulogy.

The following year, Clint Eastwood and Meryl Streep would incarnate Kincaid and Francesca for all the world. He, not the slightest bit hippie; she, not the slightest bit Italian. But what does the length and colour of your hair matter, anyway, when a simple kitchen spark can propel you halfway around the world?

"What's my surprise?"

"How'd you like to go to Mexico?"

"Yeah! And can I get a piña cola with crushed ice?"

"Okay."

"And a tiny folding umbrella?"

"You're a lucky girl. I brought some back from the restaurant this weekend."

"I hate your new restaurant."

"You always say that when things are new. You'll get used to it."

"And I wanna cherry in it... please."

"Okay, here's the deal: I'll put sugar around the edge of the glass, plus an umbrella..."

"On the side! I don't wannit to get wet!"

"... an umbrella that folds on the side, and... seven maraschino cherries."

"SEVEN?"

"Seven cherries for seven out of ten."

"Wow..."

"And here, I have a new book for you."

"It looks boring."

"Why would you say that?"

"It's too long!"

"No, it's not. Plus, we'll read it together, anyway."

"No, just you."

"We'll alternate."

"Bobolink gets a turn, too."

"And Bobolink, too. We'll pull him out from under the car by his feet."

ARIELLE AARONSON left her native New Jersey in 2007 to pursue a diploma in Translation Studies at Concordia University in Montreal. She holds an M.A. in Second Language Education from McGill University and has spent the past few years teaching English in the Montreal public school system and creating educational material for second language learners. She previously translated Marie-Renée Lavoie's *Autopsy of a Boring Wife* and *A Boring Wife Settles the Score* for Arachnide.